DULL
SNOW
RECEN

Another day in Dullsville. Or is it? The day began with news that the founder of the town, John Foster Dulls, was discovered dead near his telephone. Since he was ninety-six years old, most Dullsville citizens took this in stride. But you, feeling bored and isolated by the wintry freeze, suspect foul play and are determined to flush out the murderer despite the inclement weather.

You are the detective in this unique reader participation murder mystery. Because of the blizzard, your only means of communication is the telephone. Ten phone calls could lead you to the murderer, but can you make the right ones? Like a maze twisting through the phone network itself, the facts are hidden among false leads and dead ends, wrong numbers, busy signals, and bad connections.

So be on your guard, listen carefully, and see if you can solve the mystery of...

A CALL FOR MURDER

A CALL FOR MURDER

Alan Robbins

BALLANTINE BOOKS • NEW YORK

Library of Congress Catalog Card Number: 88-91965

ISBN 0-345-35220-3

Manufactured in the United States of America

First Edition: September 1988

Contents

How to Read This Book

The pages immediately after the Introduction contain the Dullsville Directory. This is a phone number listing of every inhabitant, office, and business in the town of Dullsville.

When you've finished reading the Introduction, decide whom you want to call first and then consult the Directory. The listings there will give you the telephone number for that individual. This number is a two-digit exchange.

You can make the phone call by looking up the two-digit exchange in the rest of the book. These numbers appear in the upper right-hand area of the pages, in consecutive order.

After each phone call, return to the Directory and decide whom to call next. Listen carefully to what people tell you in each conversation, then try to make further calls that will elicit more clues—but watch out for multiple listings, business and home phone numbers, and the usual puzzlements of any phone book.

It is possible to solve this mystery with only ten phone calls, but they have to be the right ones. You may want to look through the Directory once to familiarize yourself with the listings. As you proceed through the book, it may help to write a number next to the calls you make so that you can keep track of your progress. When you think you have a solution, call the sheriff at 99.

But remember: that phone call will disclose the answer, so don't call the sheriff until you're sure you've solved the mystery yourself.

Introduction

Sitting at the window watching the snow, you find yourself praying for a murder. If only a body were buried beneath the glistening whiteness, then you would be happy. Your dream, in fact, is for parts buried separately, each in its own frozen drift—a bloody foot here, a blue hand there. But this, you know, is just a passing fancy. In fact, there is nothing out there, nothing but snow. The whole countryside is locked under an icy blanket from which no evil could possibly escape. Too bad, you mutter.

On the desk before you, the computer sits idly and waits for you to start typing. You should be tapping out the details of another murder plot or at least a few lines of crisp dialogue, but nothing is coming to mind. Your thoughts are as pale as a blizzard. Not even the memory of a nice loud scream can get you going, and so you stare and pick your nails instead.

The plan, which seemed so clear months ago, now appears to have been a dreadful mistake. Your cousin Edgar had called to offer you his house for the winter while he went off to Paris. It was the perfect setting for a mystery writer, he said, quiet and scenic. The town in which it was located was usually snowbound from December to April, which left plenty of time to write in peace. It seemed like a great idea back then, when you used to have ideas.

So you packed your word processor, your clothes, and five months' worth of food off to Dullsville, population 78. You made a left turn off the thruway at Exit 13, followed Route 7 into the mountains, turned right at Burger King, took the country road six miles down to the big tree, and found Edgar's place, a sweet little house facing the mountains.

It was a fine plan. But what you hadn't considered was the flexibility of your own mind, the way it would conform to its surroundings, the bumps in the cortex becoming as smooth as a snowdrift, and ideas and fantasies melting like falling flakes on a woolen sleeve. And so, two months later, there you sit, with a snowball for a brain, searching desperately for drops of blood in the ice when, suddenly, the phone rings.

"Hello there," the voice says, "how are you enjoying the snow?"

"Not," you answer.

"You'll get used to it. You'll have to." It is Myna Rowell, a close friend of Cousin Edgar's. "I hope you've got enough food for at least two or three days. It'll take that long for the plows to come in. Once they do, you'll at least be able to walk into town. I hope Edgar left his snowshoes for you."

"Food's not the problem; boredom is. Don't you start to feel a bit isolated out here, Myna?"

"Sure I do, but Frank loves it here, so I put up with it. Just make a lot of phone calls. Everyone in town loves to talk and gossip from December to April. There's nothing much else to do. In fact, I was calling to tell you the news of the day."

"More snow?"

"No, J. F. died this morning!"

"I'm sorry to hear that. J. F. is your ... dog?"

"My God, you don't know who J. F. is? I thought

everybody did. J. F. is John Foster Dulls, the founder and godfather of our little hamlet. Didn't you pass the big house on the hill when you moved in?"

"You mean the mansion near the grove?"

"That's the one. It was J. F.'s home. Around here we call it the Wide House."

"Rich man."

"Multimillionaire. He used his money to create Dullsville back in the thirties."

"What did he die of? Not the excitement."

"Old age. J. F. was ninety-six years old and he was full of contraptions—hearing aids, false teeth, pacemaker, you name it. It was only a matter of time. I just heard the news from Stevie Weeks, who heard it from Bonnie Tulle. She knows someone down at the sheriff's office. J. F.'s assistant called the office this morning to say that the old man died at 8:34. What a pity."

"And how do they know he died at 8:34?" you ask, sniffing around the ingredients of the story for some spice.

"I suppose because he was constantly monitored for all those medical devices. He had a full-time doctor up at the Wide House who looked after him. It wasn't exactly a great shock. It was just bad timing for him, that's all."

"Why is that?" you ask, idly tapping the name John Foster Dulls onto the computer screen.

"He was planning to call in his vote at nine o'clock this morning. It was an important vote for the interests of the Dulls estate."

"Vote?"

"Didn't you read the last issue of *The Town Crier*?"

"I've been a bit too busy writing," you say, enclosing the name Dulls in a dagger you have drawn on the computer screen in dust.

"Oh, that's right, you're a mystery writer. Edgar told me. Then I must be interrupting your work with this silly gossip—"

"No, *no*! Please, I'm *very* interested. Go on."

"Well, the town council voted yesterday on whether to allow a major phone company to come into Dullsville and take over our little phone system here . . ."

"Take it over from whom?"

"From J. F., of course."

"John Foster Dulls owned this phone system?"

"Sure did. He owned most of the services in town. Didn't you see the signs in town for Dulls Propane, Dulls Firewood, Dulls Gas & Electric?"

"Liked to be in control of things, did he?"

"Well, yes, you could say that. He was very paternal about Dullsville. After all, it was his creation. He was a fanatic about keeping this town small and quaint."

"So what was the vote all about?"

"The town council was split right down the middle on whether to allow the big phone company in. Three in favor, three opposed. As usual, it was a deadlock. Well, when the council is split, as it always is, there's only one person with the deciding ballot."

"Let me guess ... old J. F.?"

"Right! He was supposed to call in his deciding vote this morning at nine A.M., but he up and died instead."

"Why was he calling in his vote?"

"When there's a blizzard, everything in town is done over the phone. Traveling's just too difficult. Besides, he hadn't left his house in years. Anyway, it was no big mystery how he was going to vote."

"Sure, he was going to vote against the takeover because it meant he would lose control of the telephones."

"Well, that's one way of looking at it. But I think he was just nostalgic. He wanted Dullsville to stay just the way he made it, a typical small town. That's its charm, don't you think? The town council is always split on this issue. Half of them want changes, the other half don't. It's the same deadlock every time, just like the vote allowing snowmobiles and the one on TV satellite dishes. And J. F. always broke the deadlock the same way."

"Because he was an autocratic tyrant?"

"No. Because he had a vision of a quiet little town protected from outside turmoil. Take the phones, for example. It's easy to call anyone in town using two numbers. But if you want to call out of town, you have to dial the operator, which kind of discourages outside calls. See what I mean?"

You do see. In fact, your mind has perked up and taken on some local color. You have even typed a few more names onto the computer screen: the Wide House, Bonnie Tulle, Stevie Weeks, and so on. The blank screen, bane of blocked writers everywhere, is no longer blank! It is filled with the details of your urgent wish that someone killed John Foster Dulls.

"Myna," you blurt out without thinking, "John Foster Dulls was murdered!"

"Ooh!" she hoots like a wounded owl, "what on earth makes you say a thing like that? That's absurd."

"Somebody killed the old man so that he wouldn't call in his vote."

"But why would you get such an idea?"

"Because I deserve a lucky break, that's why."

"You're writing a little mystery story here, aren't you? But I'm afraid no one would have wanted to kill old J. F. Everybody in town admired him. He was like a grandfather to us. J. F. *was* Dullsville. You could call every single person in Dullsville and you'd get the same response."

"I may have to do just that. It's all too neat—the vote, the death, the timing. I know a good plot when I see one."

"Don't be silly. He had a private physician and a nurse at his side day and night up at the Wide House. They said it was a heart attack. I should think they would know, don't you?"

"We'll see."

"Well, if you find your murderer, don't tell me about it. I wouldn't want to know. It's too depressing. Just call Sheriff Shaffer with your story; the number's in the book. I'm sure the sheriff would be very interested. Just think, Edgar's down in Atlanta soaking up the sun and missing all this excitement."

"Atlanta? Edgar told me he was going to Paris."

"Oh, he is in Paris. But he had to come back for two weeks to go to a convention in Atlanta with Marty Wince. Listen, dear, I've got to call a few other folks with the news. That's the way it works around here, the old grapevine. Bye ... and happy hunting."

Your prayers have been answered. You hang up the phone, quickly take out the Dullsville Directory, and place it on the desk like a treasure chest. Somewhere between the covers of this simple telephone book is the solution to the murder of John Foster Dulls. You are convinced of it. But for the moment, who to call, what questions to ask, and how to get answers provide a much greater mystery. The people in town don't know you and have no reason to confide in you. Then you realize that you can use this very fact to your advantage since, over the phone, you can take on any role you want.

And so, lining up bogus characters like guests at a mystery dinner, you look through the Directory and plan your attack. When you are all done, you will make one simple phone call to the sheriff—to explain your theory. But until then, the pure white landscape has taken on a deliciously sinister tinge.

The
Dullsville Directory

02

"Hey there, everybody. This is Uncle George down here at GEM Hardware where hardware becomes easy-ware with our new low, low prices on everything from Arb tools to Zink screening. It's been some winter for those of you in the frozen northeast, and GEM will be back to help you dig out from under with a special sale on Spitz snowblowers starting at $145. That's right, folks, for only $145 you can slice a path down to 22 Main Street here in Dullsville and check out Uncle George's low, low prices on ladders, hammers, paint, and pliers. We'll be open again for business on April fifteenth and look forward to seeing you with a long list of spring fix-up supplies. Thanks for calling GEM Hardware, where hardware wears hard."

05

"Hello?"

"Hello. I'd like to speak to Lucy Sparks."

"This is Lucy Sparks Shaffer. Can I help you?"

"Are you any relation to Grover Sparks?"

"Who is this? What do you want?"

"I'm with the district attorney's office in Cityville," you say, practically reading from your script. "We're checking into the possibility that descendants of Grover Sparks may have legal claims to the J. F. Dulls estate."

"Hah! That'll be the day. My brother would love to hear that one."

"So you *are* Grover Sparks's sister."

"So what?"

"Well, if you could give us a little information, we might be able to help you."

"Look, do you know how many lawyers I've seen since 1940? I could go to law school based on what I've found out about contracts and how to screw someone out of their rights. Pardon my language."

"Screw someone? Do you have some kind of grievance against J. F. Dulls?"

"J. F. Dulls ruined my brother. He stole everything Grover ever had—his ideas, his fortune, his rights. Every single patent on my brother's inventions is registered in the name of John Foster Dulls. Doesn't that tell you something?"

"Are you suggesting that he robbed your brother of his . . ."

"I'm not suggesting. I'm *telling* you J. F. Dulls was a thief and a swindler. He sucked my brother dry and got rid of him when he was through. I say thank God he's dead and can't do any more harm. And I'm not the only one who wishes they could have pulled the plug on old J. F.!"

"I thought everyone loved Dulls."

"Everyone *said* they loved him, sure. But they were really just afraid of him. If you didn't do exactly what he wanted, you might just find yourself without electricity for a week or two, or that your propane deliveries were being delayed. He had a stranglehold on this town. Did you know that a member of the town council who voted against him a few years ago was found dead in his home from gas poisoning? Suicide they called it, cabin fever. I call it a little gift from Dulls Propane!"

"You think that J. F. Dulls actually had someone killed?"

"Are you kidding? That was his biggest hobby. Go ask Lee Beagle about it."

"If this is true, then do you think someone might have murdered J. F.? In revenge?"

"I don't like to think about it. It makes me feel too sad that I didn't do it, for Grover."

"Don't feel too bad. You couldn't have anyway. He was under constant medical surveillance."

"Where there's a will, there's a way, my dear. I've stayed up many nights figuring out ways to pay off the doctor or to rig the equipment. Benny came up with twenty different ways to do it and he had no reason to hate J. F. like I do."

"Who's that?"

"Benny Firestein. He's a writer who lives in town, writes for science magazines. He knew how it could be done." There is a long pause while Lucy Sparks Shaffer reconsiders the impression she is giving. "Look, no one really killed J. F. You're just listening to decades of rage and fantasy. If you want a murderer, just call up the Wide House. That's where you'll find one. Unfortunately, he won't be able to confess much anymore. Listen, I've got to go. Doc Stone told me not to get upset and I always do when I think of how Dulls destroyed my brother's life. Wouldn't you?"

"Yes, of course. I'm sorry."

"If you need me for anything else, you know where I am. Sorry I can't be of more help."

"That's okay," you say. "I understand your feelings. What was the name of that writer again?" But you are answered only by a soft buzz.

07

"Hello?"

"Is this Agnes Mulltown?"

"Speaking."

"This is Earp from the Cityville sheriff's office—"

"Well, it's about time you people called. I've been at my wit's end all day about this horrible crime. I've called Sheriff Shaffer repeatedly and I've called the state police, and I don't know what else to do."

"Calm down, Mrs. Mulltown. We'll get to the bottom of this."

"It's Miss Mulltown. Now, are you sending troopers up here to put this man in custody or not? You'd better watch your step. He's murdered before and he'll do it again. The man is a maniac and a menace. He has a whole house full of guns and bows and arrows and things."

"Let's start from the top, Miss Mulltown. You're referring to a man named..."

"Wendell Gates...that's G-a-t-e-s. I live half a mile

from his house up here on Country Pass. I've lived in terror ever since he moved in. I knew something like this would happen, I just knew it. I saw the whole thing. It was cold-blooded murder."

"How could you see it from half a mile away?"

"Well, you see, I have a telescope that my Cousin Lea sent to me from New York. So I could watch the stars. But I also used it to keep an eye on Mr. Gates because I was certain that one day his mind would snap and he would commit some hideous crime. And I was right."

"And what exactly did you see?"

"I saw him throw the poor darling out into the snow and close the door. He knew it would freeze to death and indeed it did."

"It?"

"And then he took that poor frozen body, with its tongue sticking out like a Popsicle, and went up to Foster Lake with it. I'm sure he threw the body into the lake to dispose of the evidence. It's horrible."

"I'm not sure I'm following you on this, Miss Mulltown. Who exactly did Wendell Gates murder?"

"His dog, of course. Mind you, I hated the creature, too. It was disgusting and drooled all over the place and ate my beautiful vegetable garden, cabbages and all. But I still don't think that's any reason to kill it like that, in cold blood, so to speak."

"You're right there, Miss Mulltown. We'll take care of it, you can rest assured. Now, why don't you tilt your telescope back up to the stars and forget this whole sorry incident."

"Well, I'll certainly try. But it has been a most unsettling day, that's for certain. First that horrible man murders his dog and then poor J. F. Dulls is murdered. Just horrible. What's this town coming to?"

"Thanks for your help and... *Did you say murdered?*"

"Everyone knows that. He was poisoned. It had to happen sooner or later."

"And does everyone know who murdered him?"

"Of course. But you're the police. You must know who did it."

"Who might that be, Miss Mulltown?"

"Stevie Weeks, naturally. It had to happen sooner or later."

08

"Huh?"

"Is this Thomas Wordwood?"

"Yuh."

"Are you a reporter for *The Town Crier*?"

"Whatimezit?"

"Excuse me?"

"Is it nine yet?"

"It's noon."

"Oh, God. I guess I overslept. I'll try to make it in by three, boss. I'll just bring my things and sleep over. Sorry."

"This isn't your boss. I just need some information."

"What kind of information?"

"About J. F. Dulls, about Dullsville, about a man named Grover Sparks."

"Sparks, huh? There's a neat little tale. What do you know about him?"

"That J. F. Dulls's fortune was built on his ideas and that he never earned a penny from any of his inventions."

"That his whole family," Wordwood adds, "was mysteriously killed just as he was about to consult a lawyer about it? Strange coincidence, don't you think? And Sparks was just one of the people Dulls crushed on his way to the Wide House. I've got a dozen stories like that, but of course *The Town Crier* won't print it. If they did, Dulls would put them out of business like that."

"What else do you know about Grover Sparks?"

"Nobody knows much of anything about him, except that he was a genius. Why don't you just call up his sister? She'd know more than anyone. She lives up on Laurel Drive. I think her name is Shaffer now."

"Thanks! You've been a big help."

"Sure, sure. What's your interest in these old stories anyway? You a writer?"

"I am, actually. I'm looking into J. F. Dulls's secret past."

"Exposé?"

"Murder mystery."

"Oh, fiction. Well, don't use his name. He'll sue you down to your underwear. He doesn't like publicity."

"Not much he can do about it now."

"He's got a lot of ways of influencing people, believe me."

"From the grave?"

"Huh?"

"He died this morning. Didn't you know that?"

"*What?* J. F. Dulls? Died? Are your sure? *The* J. F. Dulls? He died this morning? Christ! I've got to get into the office. White'll kill me! It's the Dullsville story of the century, and I *overslept!*"

09

"This is a recording for the Town Hall of Dullsville. There is no one in the office at present. The office will be open again beginning April fifteenth. Please listen carefully to the following information. If you have further questions, call Dorothy Page at the library during the week. That number is 54. This tape will not accept messages. Thank you.

"The Department of Records and Documents of Dullsville is open to the public between the hours of noon and four o'clock weekdays, except during the winter months. We regret that we cannot process telephone requests regarding this information. Lake passes will be available beginning on May first at this office. The spring picnic is scheduled to take place, weather permitting, on Sunday, May third. The town council of Dullsville will meet next, in person, on Wednesday, April seventeenth. Currently under consideration are proposals for construction of a playground in the lot near Lang's TV & Radio, a new billing method for Dulls Gas & Electric, and the proposed takeover of Dulls Telephone Company by the Intercity Phone Network. The emergency plowing number is Cityville 716, twenty-four hours every day. For medical emergencies please dial 49. This is the local exchange for Cityville Central Hospital. For current emergency snow or road conditions, please call *The Town Crier* at number 53. Thank you."

10

"Hello. Elmira Hobswerth speaking."

"Hi, this is Bachman from Bachman, Brackman, and Glick in Cityville. We're trying to get in touch with an Edwina Hobswerth. Do you know her?"

"Oh, yes, that's my sister-in-law. May I ask what this is in connection with?"

"Oh, nothing important, really. Thanks a lot . . ."

"It's J. F. Dulls's murder, isn't it?"

"What?"

"I knew it! It's finally all caught up with her. All those years of covering up for him, and now that he's been murdered, it will all surface, just like on the five o'clock news."

"Who did she cover up for?"

"Why, J. F. Dulls, of course. He must have been stealing that poor Mr. Sparks blind. Edwina was his secretary. She *had* to know what was going on. Now that he finally killed him, Edwina's role in J. F.'s sordid affairs will come to light."

"Now that *who* finally killed him?"

"Why, Dr. Barton, of course. His physician. Everyone knows that J. F. rewrote his will to leave everything to Barton. In payment for his years of keeping the old crook alive. I just hope the whole thing blows up in their faces."

"Whose faces?"

"Oh, dear, dear, you're not following a single bit of this, are you? Dr. Barton and Edwina Hobswerth are brother and sister. Dr. Barton had himself written into the will, then killed J. F. with some undetectable poison so that he and Edwina would benefit from the estate. It's really quite simple."

"How do you know all this?"

"Because a very similar case was on *Murder, She Wrote* last week."

"I see."

"Now if I were you, I'd present Dr. Barton with the facts and wait for his confession. Then call Edwina and tell her Barton's confessed. She'll break down, too, and you'll have your case, all neat and tidy."

"That's great. Thanks for your help."

"Oh, it's nothing. I'm glad to get her in jail, where she belongs. She's made my brother's life miserable for the last twenty years. It's the least I can do."

11

"'Lo?" says a voice after the phone has been ringing for ten minutes.

"Hello, is this Cleve?"

"Yuh."

"Well, Cleve . . . it's Cleveland, isn't it? Mr. Cleveland?" you ask, trying to squeeze out any information you can. But your ploy is met with complete silence and you soon realize that you are going to have to put out information to get some in return. "I'm from the Intercity Phone Network. As you know, our company is planning to take over the Dullsville Telephone Company. You have heard those rumors, haven't you?"

"Yuh."

"Good. Now then, as you may know, John Foster Dulls died this morning before he could deliver his vote to the town council regarding our takeover, so it looks like we will, in fact, be moving into Dullsville. We were wondering, Mr. Cleveland . . ."

"Cleve."

"Yes, Cleve. We were wondering how you felt about this? Are you in favor of this change?"

"Favor?"

"Yes, are you happy about it?"

"Sure."

"Because . . ."

"Good for the town."

"Could you speak up a bit?"

"It's good. Johnny's gone. Now the town can breathe."

"Johnny? You mean J. F. Dulls. You feel that he kept a bit too much control over Dullsville, don't you? Well, you're not alone. According to Lucy Shaffer, John Foster Dulls had a terrible stranglehold—"

"You talk to sis?"

"Sis? Your sister?"

"Lucy."

"Lucy Sparks Shaffer! Yes, some of our people did talk to her and she said that J. F.'s passing was the best thing that could happen to Dullsville. You feel that way, too, don't you, Grover?"

It had been just a frail idea, a weightless notion, until the last fact landed in place with a thud. Cleveland was none other than Grover Cleveland Sparks himself, living in shame and anonymity above the phone company he helped to create. He hadn't run away from the town after the accident; he had simply picked a hidden spot from which to watch over it. Watch and listen, tapping into the town's conversations, keeping an open ear. That was how he knew all about the council vote and the pacemaker. It all made sense now, but you needed one final piece of confirmation. And this last piece was going to take some ingenuity to extract.

"Grover . . ."

"Name's Cleve."

"Yes, Cleve, the real reason we're calling is that we'd like to offer you a job with our company. We've heard that you're quite an electronics genius."

"Who said?"

"Lots of folks. We could use someone with your knowledge of phones and electronics. Not just in Dullsville but throughout the state. We've got new devices and inventions going in every day. Take today, for instance. We're installing three Telepulse machines in three different counties. These machines help to save lives using the phone system. They're incredible ... plug them in, start the monitor, out goes the signal at 4 kilohertz, back comes lifesaving data from a central computer. It's an exciting new world out there, Cleve, and you could be part of it."

"3.627."

"What was that?"

"4,000 cycles is trouble. Too much noise. You want 3.627 kilos."

"See that? That's exactly what I'm talking about, that expertise you have. Can we count on you to work with us?"

"Nope."

"Well, why don't you give it some thought? We'll contact you when we get into town and we can talk it over."

"Ain't int'rested."

"Well, all right, Cleve. Thanks for your time. Nice talking to you."

And with that, the final piece slips into place and it is time to call the sheriff with your theory about the unique way in which J. F. Dulls was murdered.

12

"Stop calling me, Lee. This is ridiculous. Someone is going to overhear us and we'll be in big trouble. Now, look, just stay calm and pretend nothing has happened. Let things work themselves out. If you keep calling me, someone's bound to get a party line and hear our plan. Everyone in Dullsville is on the phone this morning. Now just stay calm and relax. We'll get our money, I promise you. There's no way J. F. is going to come back as a ghost and check the books. I've got it all worked out. Okay?"

"Uh . . . hello?"

"Who is this? Lee? Is this Lee?"

"Not exactly."

"Jesus!"

"Is this the Dulls Gas & Electric Company?" you say as sweetly as possible.

"No!" says the sourpuss at the other end, just before slamming down the receiver. Repeated calls to the same number only lead to a string of useless busy signals.

13

"Hello, Dulls Propane."

"I'd like to speak to Billy Evans, please."

"Billy's out on a job right now. Can I help you? Are you having gas problems?"

"No, this is a personal matter. Is there some way I can get in touch with him?"

"Well, he's up at the Arlen place fixing a leak. But after that I think he'll be going home. He didn't feel too well today. Of course, he left before we got the news about J. F. That'll make him feel better."

"How's that?"

"Oh, nothing, just a joke."

"Would he be home yet?"

"Let's see . . . it's only noon. I don't know; it's hard to say how long the repair might take. He's either still up at Dan Arlen's, hiking through the fields in the freezing cold and cursing, or back home taking a hot bath. Take your pick."

15

"This is a recording for the Town Hall of Dullsville. There is no one in the office at present. The office will be open again beginning April fifteenth. Please listen carefully to the following information. If you have further questions, call Dorothy Page at the library during the week. That number is 54. This tape will not accept messages. Thank you.

"The Department of Records and Documents of Dullsville is open to the public between the hours of noon and four o'clock weekdays, except during the winter months. We regret that we cannot process telephone requests regarding this information. Lake passes will be available beginning on May first at this office. The spring picnic is scheduled to take place, weather permitting, on Sunday, May third. The town council of Dullsville will meet next, in person, on Wednesday, April seventeenth. Currently under consideration are proposals for construction of a playground in the lot near Lang's TV & Radio, a new billing method for Dulls Gas & Electric, and the proposed takeover of Dulls Telephone Company by the Intercity Phone Network. The emergency plowing number is Cityville 716, twenty-four hours every day. For medical emergencies please dial 49. This is the local exchange for Cityville Central Hospital. For current emergency snow or road conditions, please call *The Town Crier* at number 53. Thank you."

16

"Parts."

"Is this AA Electrical Parts?"

"You got it."

"Is there someone there who knows anything about a machine called a Telepulse?"

"Some kind of toaster?"

"No, no. It's a heart machine."

"Harp? You mean an electronic keyboard?"

"No, heart! You know . . . the kind that beats."

"I'm afraid I don't get you. What do you need, a new plug or something?"

"Look, it's called a Telepulse. It attaches to some-one's pacemaker and regulates their heartbeat."

"Nah, we only sell parts here. I got toaster parts, some keyboard parts, refrigerator, electric trains. I got any kind of motor you want: lawnmower, tractor, juicer."

"I don't want to buy anything. I need advice. Is there anyone else in town who would know about electronic things?"

"Let's see . . . you got Eddie Macon up there at Bolt Electronics, you got Larry Lang at Lang's TV. There's always my cousin Wilmer . . . he can fix anything that's got wiring in it. He's laid up with the croup though. Say, what's the name of that gizmo again . . . a Telepass?"

"Telepulse."

"Maybe I should stock up on them. You think folks'll be buying them up like they're buying VCRs?"

"Not likely, but thanks for your help."

18

The phone at the Historical Society rings for a long time without being picked up, but, determined to get a history of J. F. Dulls and the town, you relentlessly hang on and hope for the best. Eventually, someone does answer but not the fount of information you hoped for.

"There's no one here. Why do you let the phone keep ringing? I'm trying to get some sleep."

"Who is this?"

"This is Tim. Who is *this*?"

"I'm trying to reach the Historical Society. Isn't this the right number?"

"Yep. But there's no one here. What do you want?"

"I need information about the late J. F. Dulls."

"Late, is he? What do you know. All that fancy machinery couldn't keep him alive until Judgment Day."

"Look . . . when does the Historical Society meet?"

"Twice a year. You missed them by about four months. Try again in April."

"Do *you* know anything about J. F. Dulls?"

"Nope, can't say that I do. I'm just the caretaker of the building. Live upstairs and come down once a day to stoke the firebox, that's all."

"Do you know a man named Marty Wince?"

"I ought to. He and Ed Poole *are* the Historical Society."

"Well, how can I get in touch with him?"

"Try his home or you could try the library. He sometimes works out of there. Come to think of it, though, I vaguely remember Marty saying he was off on a trip this month. Could be wrong though. You say J. F.'s dead, huh? Guess we'll be getting some changes in town. Well, nice talking to you."

20

"John Foster Dulls's residence. May I help you?"

"You sure can. This is Dr. Kildare from Cityville Central. I need some information—stat!—about Mr. Dulls. We've got another patient with a very similar medical situation and we need to find out—"

"Are you, indeed? Doctor, my foot!"

"Sorry, I'm not a foot doctor, I'm a surgeon. Now, look, I want you to tell me everything you can about—"

"Far from sounding medical, you impostor, you seem to have the cackling voice of a cub reporter, in which case I have nothing to say to you or to any of your ilk."

"Reporter? Look, buster, I didn't take time off from a delicate triple bypass to pussyfoot around with you on the phone. Now I need some data and I need it fast. Every detail you can remember about J. F.'s death. You don't want another heart attack on your hands, do you?"

"You say your patient has a similar medical situation?"

"Down to the capillary, *amigo*. The details of J. F. Dulls's heart attack could save this guy's life."

"If you know that their situations are so similar, then you must know Mr. Dulls's situation quite well, and if that is the case, then you don't need any further information from me. Good day!"

"All right, pal. It's on your conscience. I'll just have the coroner write down as the cause of death 'snooty butler.' Come to think of it, the attorney general should be real interested in your reasons for withholding lifesaving information. What's going on there exactly, something shady about J. F.'s exit?"

"Good Lord, you are a pest! If you have some need of medical information, why don't you just call Mr. Dulls's private physician and see if he'll give you the data you need? The number is in the book. Now be a good little reporter and stop these shenanigans, go report to your chief—or whoever it is you people report to—and *buzz off!*"

21

"Dr. Barton's office."

"Is the doctor there?" you ask, trying to sound offi-
cious. "I'd like a word with him."

"I'm sorry, but—"

"He'll want to speak to me. This is Kranz," you say,
struggling with a faint German accent that you hope will
add authority to your voice. "I'm calling from the county
coroner's. We've just got a few questions about the late
John Foster Dulls."

"I see. Well, let me check to see if he's still in the
office."

Your goal is to find out as much as you can about the
circumstances of J. F. Dulls's timely death without giving away the charade. And so, during the interval, you
study your reflection in the window, trying to adopt an
air of old-world authenticity.

"Dr. Barton speaking, can I help you?"

"Yes, Doctor, good morning! I have a few questions
pertaining to the death of J. F. Dulls, which, we have

been informed, occurred at 8:34 this morning. If you wouldn't mind answering?"

"That was only a few hours ago. You found out pretty quickly. From the sheriff's office, I assume?"

"Yes, quite. When someone of J. F. Dulls's reputation passes on, the word does get around. Now, if you wouldn't mind giving me the details of his death, so we may complete our files . . ."

"You already have all the details, medically speaking. Mr. Dulls suffered a heart attack this morning at 8:34, from which he did not recover."

"8:34? How can you be so precise? Was someone in the room with him?"

"No, but he was being monitored for a pacemaker, so we know exactly when he died."

"You mean the old man . . . that is, Mr. Dulls . . . was hooked up to some sort of apparatus at the moment of his death?"

"Telepulse."

"I beg your pardon?"

"He was attached to a Telepulse. You're not a doctor?"

"No, clerk."

"Oh. Well, you see, Mr. Dulls had a pacemaker implanted about three years ago. Every morning he was attached to a machine called a Telepulse that transmitted information about its operation, along with heart rate, blood pressure, and so on to the Cityville Central Hospital in Cityville. It was a routine procedure."

"This Telepulse transmitted the information how?"

"Over the phone lines. Then, if any microadjustments need to be made in the pacemaker, a signal is sent back to the Telepulse from the hospital's computer. It's a very sophisticated system and quite automatic. The whole procedure takes only twelve minutes, from 8:30 to 8:42 each morning. There's no need for anyone to be in the room with the patient at the time. But what does all this have to do with the coroner's report?"

"Records are records, Dr. Barton. And Mr. Dulls simply had a heart attack during this procedure?"

"Technically, I believe there was a heart block—

which means that the heart stopped beating. The pacemaker should have been activated to stimulate the beat. Whether it did so properly or not is impossible to say. But let's face it, the man was almost one hundred years old. A pacemaker can keep you alive, but it can't make you immortal. Is that all? I have work to do."

"One last question, Doctor. Is this Telepulse system completely safe? That is, would it be at all possible for any...shall we say...foul play to enter the picture? I mean, could someone manipulate it to...turn it against..."

"What are you driving at?"

"Could it be used to harm the patient?"

"Look, it's a passive system. It hardly ever has to make adjustments. It's used mostly for monitoring vital signs. The guy was ninety-six years old, for chrissake. Why are you people always snooping around for bad news? Just because I've had a few malpractice cases, you think I've always got something to hide! That Winston Deluge case was all trumped up!"

"Calm yourself, Doctor."

"Look...Dulls was a sick old man. All the money in the world can't change that. The best technology on earth couldn't have saved him. He knew that better than anybody. So why don't you just file your report under *N* for natural causes? I've got work to do!"

"Why would he have known that better than anybody?"

"Do your own homework. You want a history lesson? Go call Marty Wince!"

"Who?"

"The town historian. Now leave me alone!"

The slam of the phone startles you, but when you regain your composure, you realize that his prescription is right. You *could* use a little background information on J. F. Dulls and the town he started. And so, back to the Directory.

22

"Hello, hello? Pinky? Pinky, is that you? I've been trying to call you for three hours. Who were you talking to? I told you not to talk to anybody. You've got to stop everything. You won't believe what's happened."

"This isn't Pinky."

"It isn't? Oh, God! I'm such a mess. This office has been in turmoil since 8:34. I don't know what I'm saying. I think I have a Valium here somewhere. Where is it? Oh, my God, who is this? Who am I talking to? Who are you?"

"It's Pinky's cousin," you bluff boldly.

"Have you spoken to him this morning? Oh, God, what's happened to him? His phone has been busy all morning. I told him not to talk to anybody; maybe it's off the hook. What am I going to do? I have to go over to the the main house and take care of things. I've *got* to get in touch with Pinky. Listen, are you going to speak to him this morning, I mean, soon?"

"Sure."

"Please give him this message. Tell him that J. F. died

this morning, that he had a heart attack and died! Tell him not to do anything! Did you hear me? He's got to call it off! His uncle died of a heart attack. Tell him Greta said not to do anything! Oh, God!"

"What's Pinky's number again?"

"It's 47 . . . or is it 74? Oh, God, I can't remember. I'm such a wreck! Look it up. How many Pinky Dulls do you think there are in the book?"

"Greta, about J. F.'s death—"

"What? J. F.? Look, you'll have to call the main house. I've got to go. He's got to stop it before it's too late. *Oh, God!*"

23

The phone at the stable rings relentlessly for ten minutes. You are beginning to doze off under the hypnotic throb of the buzz when suddenly the phone is removed from the hook. You can hear the receiver at the other end of the line hitting against three hard surfaces, as though it had been dropped. No voice answers the call, but after some concentration, in the background you can make out the sounds of the stable: a swinging door on a rusty hinge, the hoof of a horse knocking against a wooden partition, the rustling of hay. After a few moments, there is a peculiar scratching noise over the line that, your intuition tells you, may be the exact sound a horse makes when licking the receiver of a telephone.

24

"Dulls guest house."

"Hello, who is this?" you insist.

"Who is *this*?"

"This is Pollack," you bark, quickly grabbing an identity. "I'm coming over to repaint the guest house. It's supposed to be empty."

"Repaint? Now? In the middle of winter?"

"That's right. Now who are *you*?"

"Um...uh...I'm..."

"Who is it, Cleve?" says a woman's voice from the background. The man who is on the phone with you covers the mouthpiece to talk to her, but through the muffler of his palm you can still hear their conversation.

"It's someone coming to paint," he says.

"That's ridiculous. Who would authorize that? J. F. is dead," she answers.

"How the hell should I know? You better get dressed."

"My God, what if it's Clark? What if he found out? He'll kill us both."

"It's not Clark."

"I'm leaving. This was a crazy idea. It's been fun, Robert, but it's not worth dying for."

"Inez, wait! Damn," he shouts, then returns to you. "Hello? Sorry, there's been a bit of a mix-up."

"That's all right," you coo. "Mix-ups are my business. Get it? Mix-ups? I'm a painter."

"Yes, well . . . fine. Why don't you do what you have to do. We'll be out of here in ten minutes. I never liked the color in this place anyway. Reminds me of . . . unrequited love."

26

"Hello, is Millie Storch there?"

"Speaking."

"This is Detective Tracy of the Cityville Police," you say, tapping a phantom badge. "We're compiling a dossier on the late J. F. Dulls and we've been informed that you may have some information pertinent to our investigation."

"Well, I'll try to help you if I can."

"Were you in Sheriff Shaffer's office this morning when the news of his death came in?"

"Yes, I was."

"Can you tell me exactly what you overheard?"

"Just that he had died of a heart attack at 8:34 while he was on the phone or something."

"Or something? Can you be more specific?"

"His physician, Dr. Barton, who made the call, said that J. F. was connected to Cityville Central Hospital by phone when he died. That's all I heard."

"I see. Were you surprised by the news, Mrs. Storch?"

"No, I can't say that I was. Everybody expected Mr. Dulls to pass away at some point. He was quite old, you know."

"And how did you feel about him, Mrs. Storch?"

"About J. F. Dulls? I didn't really know him at all. I had only seen him, like most folks, at the annual picnic and sometimes on local TV."

"Would you say he was an honest man?"

"Well...let's just say he was a millionaire and he didn't get that way playing by the rules."

"All right, Mrs. Storch, let's stop playing games. What did you know about J. F.'s business dealings?"

"Nothing, really, nothing at all. Except all of the rumors that everyone in town has heard. That he used the town's municipal profits for his own gain, that he controlled all the services in town to manipulate people, that he was investigated by the IRS for tax fraud and the Justice Department for improper business practices. Nothing else. That's why I immediately called Stevie when I heard the news today."

"That's Stevie Weeks?"

"That's right. Stevie had been involved with J. F. on a few business deals that almost bankrupted him. J. F. was suing him, and if he won, Stevie would have been ruined. I thought he'd want to hear the good news."

"Does the sheriff know about all this? Did you tell him?"

"Everyone in town knows about Stevie and J. F. And anyway, the sheriff was busy filling out a report on Wendell Gates and didn't really have time to discuss J. F."

"What kind of report?"

"I don't really know. Agnes Mulltown had filed a complaint against Wendell Gates and the sheriff had to check into it. I only saw one entry at the top of the report."

"What was that?"

"Unlawful death."

27

Buzz, buzz, buzz, buzz. The busy signal continues for a few minutes until you come out of your stupor and hang up the phone, not quite sure what you hoped to gain by dialing your own number anyway.

29

"Bolt Electronics. We'll show you sparks!"

"What? What was that you said about Sparks?"

"It's just a motto. We change them once a week. Last week's was 'We make good connections.' I think that one was a little better. What do you think?"

"I really have no idea. Now, look, does anyone there know anything about electronics? I need some technical information."

"Well, I know something about some things. We really sell parts here, though. I could try. Tell me the problem. 'If you're in the dark, we'll shed some light.' That was three weeks ago."

"Are you familiar with a Telepulse machine?"

"Telepulse? You're in luck. I helped install one up at J. F.'s house a few years ago."

"You did? That's great. I'm from Telepulse Inc., and we're trying to gather some data on the machine."

"I thought the Telepulse was made by Medcom."

"Yes, it is. We're just a division. We're doing some

research and we're particularly concerned about electronic interference with the pulse."

"Why would you worry about that? The variable condenser acts as a frequency selective amplifier—"

"Whoa, excuse me, you'll have to go a little slower. I haven't the vaguest idea what you're talking about."

"You work at Telepulse and you don't know about the pulse regulator protections?"

"I'm in sales."

"Oh. Well, this stuff gets pretty complicated. Maybe we can save some time. What is it exactly that you want to know?"

"We want to know if it's possible for someone, anyone, to interfere with the signals and . . . well . . . how can I put this . . . kill the person using it."

"Sure it is."

"It is? How, exactly?"

"Well, in simple terms, you just electronically modify the adjustment signal. There are a lot of ways to do it. A sudden surge of voltage in the line could do it or interference from a radio wave source. But the machine is protected against all that. It's got delay devices, wave inhibitors, regulators, all kinds of stuff. It's a very well-designed machine. There are a lot of protections."

"Let's say somebody could bypass the protections. Is that possible?"

"Why would they?"

"Just hypothetically."

"Maybe."

"Where would that person have to be in order to bypass the protections and interfere with the signal?"

"Could actually be anywhere along the line. Are you talking about someone actually going out to *try* to interfere with the signal?"

"Yes."

"That's murder."

"Hypothetically."

"Well, it probably wouldn't be someone in the same room as the Telepulse itself. See, you'd need someone with an electromagnetic transducer and an oscilloscope who could monitor the pulse and input a false signal into the coupling device—"

"Sorry, I'm in sales, remember?"

"Well, what I mean is, the person would need a machine of their own. It would be pretty obvious. Now, if they had one, they could be anywhere along the line of the signal. Of course, that person would have to know the specific frequency the Telepulse was operating on. But you could find that out by trial and error, if you monitored it for a while."

"Frequency?"

"Yeah. See every electronic signal has a frequency. The phone lines are designed to operate at a frequency range of about 4000 cycles per second, which is enough to carry the sound of the human voice. That's 4 kilohertz, but it varies according to what sounds are being transmitted."

"That's the frequency the Telepulse uses?"

"No. The Telepulse has to be more specific than that. It uses a very narrow range, to avoid accidental interference. It's 3.627 kilohertz. You'd have to know that to be able to tune in the signal."

"Is it a secret?"

"It's not a secret. It's just not something you'd know unless you were working with the machine. You could find it out by monitoring the line. My partner, Eddie Macon, did it that way because he lost the instruction booklet when the machine first came."

"I'd like to talk to him."

"He's probably home playing with his kids. You know, it's amazing, but you're the second person this month who was interested in pulse transducers and all this stuff."

"I am?"

"Yeah. Cleve ordered a whole bunch of stuff just like what you're talking about. Said it was for his shortwave setup. Don't get many calls around here for this sort of thing."

"Who did you say that was? Cleve?"

"Yeah. He works over at the Dulls Telephone Company building in town. Caretaker or something, I think. I didn't even think he knew that much about electronics, but he ordered some pretty fancy parts. That was back in October, before the snow. Say, listen, do you guys at Telepulse need an electronics engineer? I'm really dying to get out of this shop. It's driving me crazy. You can only play so many games of Starblasters. You know what I mean? I've got a master's degree."

"I'll pass the information along to the personnel department."

"What's the big interest in the Telepulse anyway? Is Dulls giving you a research grant or something?"

"Not unless it's written into his will."

"Will? What will?"

"Didn't you hear? Dulls died this morning."

"What? You're shitting me! Why didn't anyone call me? Are you sure? Christ, I've got to go call Wendy and tell her. Maybe he left something for *us* in the will. The Bolts could use a little inheritance. I mean, I helped keep the old man alive the last few years!"

31

"Dulls Phone Company. This is the operator. May I help you?"

"Yes, I'm trying to get in touch with your custodian. A man named Cleve."

"His number is 80."

"Yes, I tried that, but there was no answer."

"I'll try it for you." There is a pause while the same useless connection is made. "That number appears to be out of service."

"It's very important that I get in touch with him. Does he have a home phone?"

"No, that's the only listing I have for him."

"Is there an unlisted number, perhaps?"

"I'm sorry. I don't have any other numbers for our custodian."

"There must be some way to get in touch with him. Can I leave a message for him with you?"

"I'm sorry, I can't take messages. If you'd like further information, you can call the main office of Dulls Telephone Company at number 77."

"Okay, thanks."

"You're welcome. And thanks for using Dulls Telephone, where the more calls you make, the happier we are."

32

"You have reached the offices of the town council of Dullsville. There is no one here at the moment to take your call. The council meets on the second Wednesday of every month throughout the year, except for December first through April fifteenth, when the meeting is conducted by a phone conference call. If you want to reach individual council members, please use the numbers listed individually in the Dullsville Directory. The current town council members are Elihu Wharfe, Willard Dulls, Stevie Weeks, Paul Hobswerth, Inez Starks, and Mavis Converse. For any further information about Dullsville events or activities, please call Town Hall, Notices, at number 15. Thank you."

33

"Yes? Hello?"

"Benny Firestein?"

"Speaking."

"Lucy Shaffer suggested that I get in touch with you..."

"She did, huh? Boy, Lucy must be tap-dancing in the snow today."

"Excuse me?"

"You know, because of old J. F. croaking and all. It's a great day for the Sparkses."

"Oh, yes, I'm sure it is. Now, then...I'm from the National Medical Consumer Safety Bureau—"

"Give me that again?"

"The NMC," you flub, trying to keep track of your own pretense. "I'm sure you've heard of us."

"Can't say that I have."

"That's all right. We'll send you a brochure. We're checking into the safety of certain medical equipment that was used in the home of J. F. Dulls. Our bureau is concerned that—"

"Oh, I guess Lucy must have told you about my Twenty Ways theory."

"Which theory is that?"

"For every way there is to keep someone alive, there are twenty ways to kill them. That's why people drop dead in hospitals all the time. And the more complicated the equipment becomes, the higher the ratio. Now take that Telepulse machine that Dulls was using. State-of-the-art super-high technology, right? Supposed to be totally safe. Passive, right?"

"Right."

"Bullshit! A machine like that is as likely to croak you as keep you breathing."

"It is? How so?"

"Well, think about it. The machine plugs into your pacemaker and monitors the pulse, then feeds the data into a computer. If the pacemaker is irregular or off pace in any way, the computer instructs the Telepulse to adjust the pacemaker electronically. Now, suppose the computer makes a mistake? We're talking microbeats here, fibrillation, heart block, cardiac arrest."

"Could the computer make a mistake?"

"Can human beings make a mistake? Human beings operate computers."

"But, as I understand it, the Telepulse was at the Wide House with Dulls and it sent and received the messages along the phone lines to and from the computer at a hospital in Cityville."

"Right. Think about that. That adds twenty-three miles of phone line each way for something to screw up...noise, voltage drains, faulty connections, God knows what. And think of all the personnel involved... Dulls's doctor and nurse, the Cityville hospital staff, the goddamn long-distance operator! Come to think of it, it's amazing Dulls lasted this long."

"You mean any one of those people could have killed him?"

"Killed? As in murdered? I'm just saying that the more elements there are, the more screwups there can be, that's all."

"But *could* someone have killed him?"

"Sure, anything's possible. All you'd have to do is interfere with the signal. A good TV repairman would know how to do that."

"Which signal?"

"Either one. If you screw around with the monitoring signal, the computer will get the wrong message. If you mess up the adjustment signal, the pacemaker will get the wrong instruction. Either way, the pacemaker'll stimulate the heartbeat at the wrong time and the result . . . bip bip bip beeep!"

"But how, exactly, could it be done? I mean, would you have to be in the room with the Telepulse or would you have to be at the hospital with the computer?"

"Beats me. I write science articles, not murder mysteries. You'd have to ask an electronics expert about that. Anything else? I should get back to work. I'm in the middle of a love story here between a cyborg and a microwave oven."

"Nothing else, thanks."

35

"Hello?"

"Is this Bert Barton?"

"Yes, it is. What can I do for you?"

"I'm calling from Cityville Central Hospital. Are you by any chance a doctor?"

"Why, are you short of staff today? How much does the job pay? For a decent wage, I'll stick needles in unconscious patients."

"No, we're not looking for doctors. We're trying to find a particular Dr. Barton."

"Oh, you're looking for Mel. That's my brother, the butcher. My mother always thought I'd make a better doctor than Mel. Clearer thinker, steadier hands. Well, it didn't work out that way. The hell with it! What do you want him for? Malpractice or involuntary manslaughter?"

"Has he been found guilty of that?"

"Oh, no, never found guilty! J. F. would never have allowed that! No, Mel just plugs along, buzzsaw in hand, and lets J. F. cover the damage. But if you're looking to hire Mel at the hospital, I'd forget that idea. I doubt that he'll be ruining people's health for much longer. Now that the old man is gone, Mel should be coming into a little cash. He'll be hanging up the shingle, thank God."

"You don't sound too happy about your brother."

"You work at Cityville? Then you've heard all the rumors that he and Vane were running a drug ring financed by J. F. Dulls. Now, is that the kind of guy you want giving you a prescription?"

"A drug ring?"

"You never heard that?"

"I just started today. Is it true?"

"Well, the state police didn't think so, but who are they compared to J. F.'s millions? The fact that someone in the hospital was ordering too many barbiturates and that they were disappearing from the dispensary that Vane was in charge of and that the number of ODs in Cityville was mushrooming and that Vane and Melville Barton were medical students together—all that somehow didn't add up to anything to the cops. I don't know, what do *you* think?"

"I think J. F. Dulls wasn't the pillar of society most people think he was."

"Hey, nobody's perfect. He donates a few dollars every year to the Daughters of the Thirteen Colonies. What do you want from the guy?"

"You say everyone at Cityville here knows about the drug business?"

"You're new there, right? You want my advice? Forget that you ever heard about it. Snooping around won't get you anywhere and you could end up under a snowplow. You want my darling brother, give him a call at the Wide House. He's probably running around stuffing bills in his pockets to celebrate. Go call him; it's number 51. And if he takes the job, just keep him away from sharp objects and he'll work out fine."

36

Alexander Graham Bell never got a busy signal. That's because Watson had no one else to call. Imagine the different course history would have taken had Watson been on the phone with someone else while Bell was trying to get through with his revolutionary message.

You, however, are not Bell and must therefore put up with the annoying realities of the busy signal. You try the number repeatedly, but always with the same grating response, the familiar beeping sound of a phone already in use. And you wonder, as you return to the pages of the Directory, if Bell couldn't have picked a more musical way to tell people to buzz off.

37

"Hello, Winston Deluge?" you bark, hoping to catch him off guard. "Hoover here, of the Governor's Malpractice Board. We need some details about Dr. Melville Barton. You were his patient once, weren't you?"

"No, my father was."

"Would you mind giving us the facts of the case? You had a malpractice suit against him?"

"No, it wasn't malpractice. It was criminal negligence. He killed my father, murdered him."

"Why would he do that?"

"Let's call the motive stupidity."

"What was the verdict?"

"The verdict? The verdict was a joke. J. F. Dulls had gotten to all of the jurors. Naturally they found for the defendant. We had expert testimony, concrete evidence —none of it mattered. Dulls knew how to control people."

"How exactly did Barton kill your father?"

"You work for the governor? Then you should be able

to find out for yourself. The governor was Dulls's pal, wasn't he?"

"This is an independent investigation, Mr. Deluge, conducted under the auspices of the...um...federal ...attorney general's office."

"He gave my father an overdose of a drug called theophylline, for emphysema. My father was a chronic smoker. A first-year medical student would know the right dosage, but not that quack. The overdose killed him. Period."

"An accidental overdose?"

"Unless he was hoping to inherit my father's lungs to sell to some university, it *must* have been an accident. But it was a stupid accident, for which Barton should have paid. Of course, Barton had John Foster Dulls behind him, so how could he lose? Top lawyers, jury tampering—they even tried to threaten my family to drop the suit."

"And why would Dulls give him all this help?"

"Christ, you guys don't know anything, do you? Why don't you ask Elihu Wharfe why Dulls was protecting Barton? He had plenty to say at the trial. Why don't you see how chatty he is now that his boss is dead?"

"What was that name again?" you ask, but the click has already ended your inquiry.

38

"Yes?" says a man with a deep baritone who answers the phone.

"I'm trying to get in touch with an Edwina Hobswerth. Is she at this number?"

"Just a moment. Edwina, there's a call for you!" the man says as he hands the phone over to someone else.

"Thank you, Paul. Hello, this is Edwina Hobswerth."

"Great. I'm calling from the *Cityville Examiner*. We're doing a piece on John Foster Dulls; big spread, front page. 'J. F. Dulls: The Inside Story.' See what I mean? We were told that you worked with Dulls in the beginning. Is that true, ma'am?"

"I was his secretary for a very brief period back in . . . oh, it must have been 1935 or so."

"We've heard a rumor that Dulls had actually stolen the patent rights for various inventions from a man named Grover Cleveland Sparks. Can you confirm that for us?"

"Well, I didn't know it at the time, but many years later, I realized that Mr. Dulls must have engaged in some unfair business practices. After all, he did end up with all the money."

"Why didn't you go to the authorities with this information?"

"I didn't realize it until long after it happened. Besides, it would have been fruitless. J. F. Dulls was a very clever man. It would have been impossible to prove a case against him."

"Come on, Mrs. Hobswerth. You were his secretary; you must have had some suspicions in the beginning."

"Well, there was a time back then when I suggested to Mr. Sparks that he should speak to a lawyer. But he wasn't the kind of man to do that. He was painfully shy and he trusted Mr. Dulls with everything, all the details. But then the fire happened and changed everything anyway. It destroyed Mr. Sparks and ended their association."

"You mean the fire in his lab, the one that killed his wife and child."

"Yes. Oh, it was terrible. It began in the attic apartment where Mr. Sparks worked and lived with his family. Mr. Dulls and I barely made it out of the blaze ourselves."

"Dulls was in the building during the fire?"

"Oh, yes, we both were. He had just come down from Mr. Sparks's apartment and we were going over some documents when there was a small explosion, which ignited some chemicals and started the fire. We ran out in a panic, but we couldn't get back inside to save Mrs. Sparks and little Emma. It was horrible. The building burned to the ground. After that, of course, Mr. Sparks was despondent, as you can imagine. He soon disappeared from town, never to be heard from again. It was a terribly sad time for all of us."

"Dulls had come down from Sparks's apartment just before the fire?"

"Yes. The police felt that Mr. Sparks must have left an electrical switch open that caused a spark. But, unfortunately, Mr. Dulls didn't notice it."

"Or did he?"

"I beg your pardon?"

"Nothing."

When you hang up the phone, it is with renewed admiration for the scales of justice. In all likelihood, Dulls opened the switch himself, started the fire, and killed Sparks's family. Maybe he only intended to ruin Sparks by destroying his experiments. Or maybe it was premeditated murder. Either way, the result was the same. And the reason he kept Cleve nearby all these years was to keep an eye on him in case he found out the truth.

The sheriff was right. There was no need for any kind of investigation; the verdict had already been passed. Arresting Cleve would accomplish nothing. On the contrary, he had done the town a favor. You might even suggest, along with the other changes, a new name for it. Cleveland seems like a reasonable choice.

Still, there is a feeling of sadness as you sit at the window. Not for the victims but for the story. Too bad it has to go to waste. But there, behind the phone resting quietly on its cradle, the computer screen is already filled with names and notes. Yes, perhaps the story won't be wasted after all, you decide, as you take the phone off the hook so that you won't be disturbed.

39

The ringing of the phone, at regular intervals, seems to be coming from a great distance. The sound reaches you through the hidden labyrinth of the phone system, over wires carrying private confessions and public allegations. The rhythm of the ringing brings on a kind of auditory seizure that causes you to sit, rather mindlessly, wearing the expression of an abject idiot. For a moment it seems that this stupidity is the final resolution of your little mystery tale. But this would be wrong. The meaning is clear: No one is home. There is simply no answer.

40

"Hello?"
"Is this the Arlen residence?"
"Hello?" the tiny voice says again.
"Yes, is this the Arlen house?"
"I'm Kate."
"Is your father home?"
"No."
"Is your mother home?"
"Yes."
"Can I talk to her?"
"No. She's sick."
"Oh. Is there a man there fixing the gas?"
"Yes."
"Can I talk to him?"
"No."
"Why can't I talk to him?"
"He went."
"He left?"
"He went home."
"Thanks, Kate."

"My brother Tom threw Becky into the washing machine."

"He did?"

"Yes, and he said she would drown unless I got inside with her. But Tom is stupid."

"Is Becky your cat?"

"No, silly, she's a doll. And I told Tom I would climb in, then I closed the door and then when he couldn't see, I pulled out the plug and all the water went out and then I took out Becky and dried her off."

"Very clever."

"Tom's stupid."

"Bye, Kate."

"Bye."

41

"Is Eddie Macon there?"

"I'm sorry, Eddie's out making an igloo."

"An igloo?"

"With the kids."

"Oh. Well, could you ask him to call me back when he gets a chance? I'm staying at Ed Poole's house . . ."

"You're his cousin, right?"

"That's right. I need some information about a machine that J. F. Dulls was using called a Telepulse. I thought Eddie might be able to help me out."

"I'll tell him when he gets back. Ed told us you were a mystery writer. Are you trying to figure out the mystery of J. F.'s murder?"

"How did you know that?"

"Just a guess. Half the town is on the phone this morning trying to figure out who might have killed him. And the other half is hoping they won't be suspected."

"Who do *you* think did it?"

"You don't *really* think anyone killed him, do you? It's just the day's gossip."

"I guess not. I'm really just writing a new novel, I suppose."

"In which someone uses the Telepulse to secretly knock the old man off?"

"Something like that."

"Well, Eddie's the man to ask. He installed that machine up at J. F.'s house. When he gets back...wait a minute...why don't you call the office? Phil is down there. He knows as much about it as Eddie. Yeah, call Bolt Electronics. Phil will be able to give you some details."

42

"I simply can't talk now," Myna says in an excited rush. "I've been on the phone for two hours and I haven't made Frank his lunch yet. This whole town is going bananas over J. F.'s death. Everyone thinks someone else had a hand in it. It's insane, but your hunch may have been right after all. Listen, darling, if I were you, I'd call *The Town Crier* and find out all I can about J. F. Dulls and his business associations. According to everyone I've spoken to, he wasn't completely on the up-and-up. Maybe someone really was trying to do him in. Wouldn't that be amazing? Well, I've got to go call Bonnie before I make Frank his lunch and tell her what Agnes Mulltown said. Bye-bye now. And good luck."

44

While you idly tap on the phone with a pencil stub, the ringing continues for a long time until someone picks up the receiver and replaces it, thereby disconnecting your call. After three rounds of this same game, you realize that Hillary Dill is avoiding the phone call and you abandon the effort to reach her.

45

"Dulls Firewood. Can I help you?"

"Is Mel Snitchit there?"

"No, I'm sorry. Mel is out sick today. This is his assistant, Barnaby. Can I help you with something? We've got a special on hardwood today . . . five cords for thirty dollars."

"He hasn't been in the office all day?"

"Oh, sure, he was in this morning. Packed up the truck with deliveries and everything. But then he took sick and had to go home. Poor guy, he's been a wreck this past week. He looks awful."

"Gee, that's too bad. Same old problems, huh?"

"Same old family trouble."

"Oh, that again."

"Do you know Mel?"

"Like a brother."

"Well, then, you know all about his family trouble . . . the Dulls family."

"Sure. Crazy stuff."

"Pinky's been driving him nuts, calling him all hours

of the day and night. Mel's not a well man; he needs his rest."

"So Pinky's been calling him day and night?"

"Yeah, just because Pinky's having an affair with Greta Wince, you'd think the whole world was at stake."

"That's why he's been calling Mel? Because of this affair?"

"I don't know what Pinky's up to. He's such a sleaze-bag, it could be anything. Probably some scam for stealing his uncle's estate, if I know Pinky. He thinks that just because Mel has a prison record, he'll go along with any scheme he's dreamed up. Well, Mel never tried to hide his prison record. Everyone knows about it."

"Do you think Mel is still at home?"

"Sure. But I wouldn't call him there if I were you. He looked pretty sick this morning. Say, do you know Pinky Dulls, too? Maybe you could do Mel a favor and give Pinky a call, tell him to ease off. I think Mel may be having a nervous breakdown. Hello? Hello?"

47

"Heh-heh-hello?" the voice at the other end of the line stammers nervously.

"Burnout?" you whisper.

"*Burnout*? Screw you, you bastard! Don't you know what's going on? J. F. died this morning of a heart attack! You goddamn idiot! He died, did you hear me? I never set the goddamn fire. I was waiting all morning for your stupid call, then I heard that he died and I thought that you set the fire. You knew where the gasoline was, and *you* knew which of the logs was the exploding one. So what did you need me for? I figured you were going to do it yourself, then turn me in for it. Sure, the cops would believe Pinky Dulls over an ex-con who served three years for arson. So I called the goddamn sheriff, but the line was busy. Then I heard it was a heart attack. What a joke! You've got me running around all week setting up an arson murder so *you* can run off with his money *and* his secretary—and the old man up and dies of natural causes. And now you call me with the secret word! You don't even know what's going on, you goddamn idiot!

You don't believe me, go call Dulls's doctor. He'll tell you. Dulls is dead. And I'm not taking the rap for it. I've had it, Pinky, I've had it up to here with you! Go tell the prison board about me, tell them I'm working illegally, tell them anything you goddamn want to tell them. I'm through; I've had it. Go get some other sap to carry out your idiot plans."

48

"Ya? Whaddaya want?"

"Wendell Gates?"

"Who wants to know?"

"This is Kojak . . . I mean, Komack . . . of the state police."

"So what?"

"We've gotten a report from the sheriff's office that you committed a crime . . ."

"Sure, I killed him."

"You did?"

"Sure I did. And I'd kill'm again if he came back from the dead, the bastard!"

"But why?"

"Pain in my ass, is why. Always buttin' into everyone's business, chewing up property left and right, crappin' all over th'place. The hell with'm, he was no good."

"How did you kill him, exactly?"

"Snuck up from behind when he wasn't lookin', tied the goddamn phone cord around his mouth so he couldn't take a bite outta me, and booted him out into the snow. Closed the door on'm. Oh, he wailed like a banshee for hours, but I didn't pay no mind. In the morning, when the sun come up, there he was frozen solid like an ice cube. Dropped the body into Foster Lake up there."

"Wait a minute, Mr. Gates, are you saying you dropped the frozen body into Foster Lake?"

"Damn right. That's the only burial he deserved, the mongrel. Floated, too."

"What body are we talking about anyway, Mr. Gates?"

"J. F.'s body, a'course. What the hell else?"

"You killed J. F. by throwing him into the snow?"

"I put'm outta his misery. You think he liked being the slobberin' bastard he was? I sent'm on to a better world. Maybe next life he'll come back human. I did'm a favor. Eatin' my goddamn shoes, that was the last straw."

"I beg your pardon?"

"You heard right. That old hound dog chewed up my rubber boots. I'll have t'wait three weeks t'get another pair from L. L. Bean. Well, that was it, and I just throttled'm and booted him out the door."

"J. F. . . . Dulls?"

"Sure. Named him after the old man. Cute little critter when he was a pup, but how the hell was I to know he'd turn out to be such a goddamn pain in the ass? I know, old lady Mulltown called the cops on me. The hell with her, she's just an old bitch. She's next on the list anyway. I ain't sorry I croaked the dog. You want to throw me in jail for it? So be it. But I'll be goddamned if I'm gonna apologize to you or God almighty for gettin' rid of that beast."

49

"Cityville Central, is this a medical emergency?"

"No, it isn't. I'm calling from the Dullsville sheriff's office," you say flatly. "We need some information on a patient of yours, a Mr. John Foster Dulls."

"I'll have to connect you to the main operator. This is the number for emergencies. Please hold."

While waiting, you work on your imitation of a small-town cop, sensing that your normal pitch might be a bit too frail to command respect. You know that every little bit will help since the call is a shot in the dark.

"Operator, can I help you?"

"I'm from the sheriff's office in Dullsville. We need some information on John Foster Dulls. He was one of your patients. He died this morning."

"Who was the attending physician?"

"I don't know."

"What room was he in?"

"Don't know that either."

"I'm sorry, but we've got dozens of patients here. I can't help you if you don't know his room or his doctor."

"Did you have a lot of patients drop dead this morning?"

"My records don't show any patients canceling today."

"Canceling?"

"Passing away."

"Look, J. F. Dulls wasn't *any* patient; he was the richest man in the whole state. The governor won't be too happy to find out you have no record of his biggest contributor."

"I don't see that name on my register. I'm sorry."

"Let me talk to the chief cardiologist. We'll get to the bottom of this before the governor finds out."

"All right, I'll put you through to Dr. Vane. He's our chief resident in cardiology."

Another long pause—to the tune of "Heartache Blues" in Muzak—gives you time to prepare a new, more intimidating identity.

"Dr. Vane's office."

"Is the doctor there? I have a few questions for him about one of his patients. I'm from the state board."

"Which state board?"

"The Governor's Board of Medical Ethics."

"I'm sorry, Dr. Vane is in surgery."

"When can I call back?"

"Dr. Vane won't be available until next week."

"Look, babe, I don't have time to wait for Dr. Vane to take a week in Bermuda. We've got an investigation to run. The governor is waiting for our report. Now, when does Dr. Vane get out of surgery?"

"He gets out at three o'clock, but he won't be recovered until next week."

"Recovered? Who's he operating on...the president?"

"Dr. Vane is being operated on. He's the patient. A coronary bypass."

"Oh, I see. Well, maybe you can help me."

"I'm sorry, I'm not authorized to give out any—"

"Look, kid, why don't you make it easy on yourself and your boss and just give me some information. You don't want me to have to send federal marshals down there to subpoena all of the doctor's files, do you? That would look pretty messy in the papers. Do you get my meaning?"

"Well..."

"Good. Now what do you know about John Foster Dulls? Was he Vane's patient?"

"Yes."

"He was?"

"In a manner of speaking. Mr. Dulls's physician of record was Dr. Barton, but, due to the special circumstances of his condition, Dr. Vane was consulting."

"What special conditions were those?"

"Mr. Dulls was monitored daily for his pacemaker. Every morning he was attached to a Telepulse monitor in his home, and the information was relayed to our computer here at Cityville. If any adjustments or modulations had to be made in the pacemaker, the information was sent back to the Telepulse over the phone."

"And was this procedure being done this morning?"

"Oh, yes, but it seems that Mr. Dulls had an irreversible seizure during the procedure. His line went totally flat."

"His what went what?"

"His cardiac graph went flat. His heart stopped beating."

"Just like that?"

"It happens. We tried to send a different signal to the Telepulse, but the episode was too complex to compensate for. It was too late."

"Was Dr. Vane there?"

"Oh, no, Dr. Vane was being prepped for surgery. I was monitoring it. I know the procedure as well as he does. We've been doing it every day for more than a year. Dr. Cutter was in the room, but I'm the one who really ran it."

"You didn't find anything unusual or peculiar about the whole incident?"

"Well, there seemed to be a surge of voltage just before the seizure. But that wouldn't have been enough to affect the Telepulse. Why do you ask?"

"Oh, we're just checking out every possible angle."

"Angle of what?"

"You seem like a nice nurse, Nurse, so I might as well tell you the truth. We're looking into the possibility that J. F. Dulls was murdered."

"Oh."

"You don't sound very surprised."

"Well, I know that he wasn't exactly loved by all the people in his town, but still, it would have been very hard to murder him."

"Why is that?"

"He was always surrounded by people. Dr. Barton lived on his estate and checked him a few times a day. And there were servants and assistants. How could someone have gotten in...unless..."

"Unless?"

"Unless they were all in cahoots. Do you think the whole town killed him? That would make a great movie. If I were you, I'd find out all I can about the history of Dullsville. Maybe it was a conspiracy."

"We'll see about that, Nurse. Thanks for your help."

50

"Hello, is this Ruby Gross?"

"That's me."

"Do you work for Vic Bonsalvo at Dulls Trash and Scrap?"

"Not exactly."

"You don't work for him?"

"It's more like I bust my ass for him. People who work get paid for their labor, don't they?"

"You don't get paid?"

"Minimum. Vic and me don't really get along too well. Why should we? I'm out on the damn truck all day picking up everyone's old beer cans and used toothpaste tubes. He's back in the office trying to get into Lola's pants. *Just a pair of friends*, my ass. I told his wife about them, too. The hell with him."

"I see."

"He had it in for me from day one. Just because of that stupid sign business. The sign company forgot the first letters of every word. So I put up what they gave me and for three weeks it was ULLS RASH AND CRAP. Not my fault. He thought I did it on purpose. And ever since then he's been on my back. He and his patron, Mr. John Foster Dulls."

"I'm more interested in J. F. Dulls himself. You didn't have a very high opinion of him, did you?"

"In a word...sleazebag. Did Vic tell you about my secret note?"

"Yes, the note. Tell me about it."

"Found it in the trash. Where else, right? I mean, it's not like I go through people's garbage or anything. But one day I came back to the main depot and I saw this note scrawled on a memo page. Still got it right here."

"What does it say?"

"It's a little hard to read because part of it's all slopped up from the trash. But I can still make it out. It says:

> Walter,
> Have hired Assassin.
> Go ahead with murder.
> Disposal of the stick not a problem.
>   J. F."

"Pretty interesting note," you say, writing down the words. "What do you make of it?"

"It's obvious. J. F. was planning to have someone killed. From what I hear, it wouldn't be the first time either. I told Vic about it, but he just laughed it off. He said if I caused any trouble he'd dispose of me for good."

"So you never told anyone about it?"

"No. And now that J. F. is dead, I guess it doesn't matter very much."

"Who is Walter?"

"That'd be Walter Winfle. He worked with J. F."

"Maybe I'll give him a call and ask him about the note."

"Go ahead. Just leave my name out of it. I don't want to get fired. Trash ain't much, but it's all I've got."

51

"Yes?"

"Is Dr. Barton there?"

"Who?"

"Dr. Melville Barton."

"You've got the wrong number."

"Look, this is Agent Smark from the Federal Bureau of Investigation. Why don't you save us the trouble of having to come down there in person and put Barton on the phone?"

"The FBI, huh? That's exciting. What's Barton done? I heard about J. F. Dulls this morning. Do you think Barton killed him? Ooh, I'll have to call Edwina and tell her. This is great."

"Where is Barton, miss?"

"I guess at his office. How do you think he did it? Poison? He's a doctor; he'd be able to get away with that. Maybe he drugged him. You know he was involved in a scandal at Cityville Central Hospital a few years ago about their supply of drugs. That's it, he might have drugged him to death."

"This isn't Barton's office?"

"Oh, no. This is my house."

"Are you a relative of Barton?"

"Certainly not! I wouldn't hear of having a cold-blooded killer in my family. We go back to the arrival of the *Mayflower*. Barton is an immigrant and everyone knows they're the ones who bring crime to this country."

"Who exactly are you?"

"Doris Pott. Now, if you want my advice, you won't just call up Barton and spill the beans, as they say on TV, because that will scare him off. You'd better get some more information about his shady past. Maybe there's a way you can trick him into confessing. I've seen that on *Perry Mason* a few times."

"If you're not related to Barton and you don't work for him, then why did his brother give us your number to reach him?"

"Bert gave you my number? Oh, he's always mixing things up. He has no memory at all. My theory is that he's been angry at his brother for so many years, his mind is all filled up with rage instead of ideas. Listen to me. I've got this all figured out. Why don't you call up *The Town Crier* and find out all you can about J. F. Dulls and how he started Dullsville and how he first became acquainted with Mel Barton? Build your case up from the start, do your research. Then you'll nab him. Believe me, that's how Colombo would do it. Well, good luck with your investigation. Goodbye."

53

"*Town Crier*. All the news that fits, we print. If you're calling to place a classified ad—"

"I'm not. I'm trying to get some information about J. F. Dulls. Is there anyone there who could help me?"

"I'll put you through to our editor. Maybe he can help."

Moments pass while you listen to a scratchy recording of the old standard "Call Me and I'll Be Around." Finally, a gruff voice interrupts the interlude, catching you by surprise.

"White here, what's the story?"

"Hi there! My name is ... uh ... Kent. I'm trying to get some info on J. F. Dulls, who, as you probably know, died this morning. I'd like a little background on—"

"For whom, Kent? Who do you work for? You with the *Examiner*?"

"No, no. This is purely informal. The members of the Women's Legion of Decency are putting together a little booklet to commemorate the life of J. F. Dulls and we want to make sure we've got the facts right."

"Women's what?"

"The WL of D. I'm sure you've heard of it. We had our annual luncheon in September. Now, then, could you just fill me in a bit on a little town history like how J. F. amassed his fortune and so on?"

"It's a pretty well-known story. I thought everyone knew it by now."

"We like to get things accurate."

"I understand. I wish I could get Wordwood to see it the same way. He's my reporter. Well, let's see. Dulls was a drifter in the beginning, no money, odd jobs—that sort of thing. Up until about 1930. That year sure changed his life."

"Why?"

"He met up with a man named Grover Sparks. Grover C. Sparks. He was an electrical genius, particularly in the area of communications, what they'd call nowadays a phone freak. He had all sorts of inventions relating to the telephone, but he was painfully shy, too shy to sell or to profit from his own inventions. Well, that was where Dulls came in. You sure you want to hear all this?"

"Absolutely. It's a great help."

"Dulls and Sparks formed a partnership to market these phone inventions: an amplifier to improve the sound, some kind of dial mechanism, a better ringing device—that sort of stuff. They were doing pretty well together, Sparks inventing the devices and Dulls making the deals. Then, in 1935, came a bonanza. Sparks invented an automatic switching device that eliminated the need for manual operators. They tried out the first one right here in this town. That's why we've got automatic switching even though there are only a few dozen phones in town. It was a revolution in the technology. Dulls sold the device to AT&T for a fortune, plus royalties for years to come."

"So they both became rich."

"No, because 1936 changed all that."

"The Depression?"

"The accident. You see, nobody ever saw much of Sparks because he was up in his apartment coming up with inventions. But one day Sparks left his apartment to get some parts. He must have left a switch open that caused a spark and ignited some chemicals. The whole place burned to the ground. His wife and kid, who lived up in the attic with him, were killed. He was only about twenty-five, too."

"And Dulls?"

"Out of town. A woman who worked for them, Edwina something, barely got out alive. It was a terrible blow for Sparks and it totally destroyed him. He was a very quiet, very shy man who relied on his family for strength. And he blamed himself for their deaths, even though it was obviously an accident. Anyway, Sparks disappeared after that, probably committed suicide."

"So Dulls ended up with all the money for Sparks's inventions?"

"Yup. He used it to create the town of Dullsville from the few houses that were here in the beginning. And that made him another fortune. Between all of the businesses he owned here and other investments, I'd say Dulls was one of the richest men in the state."

"What a sad story. Poor Sparks."

"Well, just don't stress that in your little booklet. After all, that accident made Dullsville possible, and we're all happy about that."

"But to have your whole family wiped out suddenly, and think it was your fault!"

"Yup. I think Sparks may have had a sister, but I never heard much about her. Guess she moved to another town after the accident. Well, is that enough for you, Kent?"

"It's great, Mr. White, you've been a lot of help. The Women's Legion of Decency will never forget you. We'll send you a copy of the booklet."

54

"Dullsville Library, Dorothy Page speaking. May I help you?"

"I'd like to speak to Marty Wince, please," you say.

"Are you leaving a joke for his book?"

"I beg your pardon?"

"Are you calling to leave a joke for his compendium, *Dullsville: A History in Humor*?"

"No, not at all. I'm calling to get some information."

"Oh, well, Marty's out of town until April. Is there something I can help you with?"

"Yes, I'm from the *Cityville Examiner*. We're trying to put together an article on J. F. Dulls."

"I told you already."

"You did?"

"You just called an hour ago, didn't you?"

"Not me."

"Well, one of the other reporters called and I told him everything I knew about J. F. It wasn't that much to begin with since I only moved here three years ago. But I've explained all that already."

"They never tell me anything around here," you explain ruefully. "I'm new and everyone takes advantage of me. Listen, would you mind just going over a few of the things you said, to make sure—"

"I really don't have the time to go into all this again. But as I told your associate, if you want information about J. F. Dulls or the town of Dullsville, the best way to find out is to call the Historical Society. Now, if you'll excuse me, I have a great deal of cataloguing to do."

56

"Stevie Weeks?"

"Yeah."

"This is Bibble from the Better Business Bureau," you stammer.

"It's about time. Now that J. F.'s gone, everyone's coming out of the woodwork to poke around. Swell, I've been on the goddamn hotseat for ten years and now that it's safe, suddenly everyone's interested in J. F.'s dealings. Christ."

"What kind of information exactly do you have?"

"Kind? What kind would you like? Do you want to start with *A* for arson or *W* for watered stock? In the middle there's *E* for extortion, *M* for murder, and *S* for general sleaziness. Take your pick; I've got a file cabinet full of details."

"Murder?"

"Okay . . . murder. Do you want negligent manslaughter like old lady Conkey or outright premeditated homicide like the Phipps kid? That one was a classic. Craig Phipps found out that J. F. was stealing from the town's charity donations and was going to go to the police with it, so J. F. managed to have his kid run over by a plow."

"How do you know J. F. had it done?"

"Come on, Dulls Mowing and Plowing? The week before Phipps was leaving for the state capital? Give me a break. I've got tons of this stuff. It's no surprise that someone killed him. I'm happy they got him before he got me."

"You realize, Mr. Weeks, that everything you've said so far makes you a prime suspect for this, don't you?"

"Me? Sure, I've got a cabinet full of reasons to have killed him, but I didn't do it and I can prove it."

"How can you prove it?"

"You tell me, how is a man in a wheelchair going to trudge up to the Wide House and murder J. F. Dulls? That's right, a wheelchair, courtesy of a bizarre accident at a construction site four years ago when J. F. Dulls and I were in business together. A tractor slipped its gear and ran over my leg. Ever hear of an accident like that?"

"No."

"Because they don't happen. But the court wouldn't see it that way and, once again, our fine Mr. Dulls got off scot free. Not to mention that business with Victor, who runs Dulls Trash and Scrap. But, look, there're maybe fifteen people in town with the same kind of stories who aren't in wheelchairs. There's no lack of suspects."

"Like whom?"

"No you don't, Bibble. I may be crippled, but I'm not stupid. How do I know you're who you say you are? I think I'll just wait for the state investigation."

"There won't be any investigation if you don't speak up. Everybody thinks J. F. died of a heart attack."

"Oh, yeah? Well, you go call his doctor and get the details of his death. I promise you, somewhere in there is a clue to the fact that he was murdered. For me, I think I'll just sit back and drink a toast to his timely demise."

57

"Walter Winfle, please."

"Howdy."

"Mr. Winfle?"

"You got'm. Now what're y'going to *do* with'm?"

"This is Pyle from the State Archives. We're going through the private papers of J. F. Dulls, which were just given to us by his estate today...."

"Holy smokes, that was a fast. The old man only kicked the bucket this morning. What'd you do, fly in a chopper to pick'm up?"

"We pride ourselves in efficiency, Mr. Winfle. Now, in going through his various documents and papers we have come across a rather curious memo that is addressed to you. We thought you might be able to help us file it properly. It says:

> Walter,
> Have hired Assassin.
> Go ahead with murder.

Disposal of the stick not a problem.

J. F."

"Well, where in holy hell did'ya get that from?"

"It was among his papers."

"That crazy old fool kept a copy? Didn't trust nobody, did he? Can't say as how I blame him though."

"You recall the note, then?"

"Course I recall the note. Keep the original in my den as a memento. That was our first deal together and we made a killing, sure as shoot. But somebody's pullin' your leg, friend. Maybe old J. F. himself from the Great Beyond."

"How's that?"

"That note's been changed."

"It has?"

"Yessiree. I got the damn original right here, framed and pressed. Mine says:

Walter,
Have hired Assassi.
Go ahead with merger.
Disposal of the stock not a problem.

J. F.

Assassi was a lawyer J. F. hired to help with the merger. We sold off the stock in the old company and the merger went through. Made a few million on that one, bless old J. F.'s heart. Cold as canyon water he was, but he knew a deal when he saw one. That note you've got there sounds like all the important words got slop all over them at the bottom of the trash pail. Hello? You still there?"

You are there, but your mind has been derailed by the foul-up. And so, it's back to the Directory to try to get back on track.

59

"Howdy-doody."

"Hello?"

"Whatkin I do fer'ya?"

"Is this Chester Sperks?"

"So my mom named me. Been livin' with it for sixty years. Named fer my pap, I was."

"Was your father's name, by any chance, Grover?"

"Yes, it was. Say, are you with one'a them there game shows? Do I win somethin' fer bein' the son of Grover Sperks? Sure could use a new snowplow."

"Sorry, I'm not giving away any prizes. I'm trying to get some information on a man named Grover Sparks who lived here a long time ago."

"How's that?"

"Sparks, with an *a*."

"Nope. What you *got* here is Chester, son of Grover Sperks with an *S-p-e*. The man you want killed himself more than thirty years ago."

"You've heard of him? You've heard of Grover Sperks—I mean, Sparks."

"Sure have. He'n my dad used to go fishin' together. That is, until that damned fire that killed his wife and kid. What'cha want t'know about, anyway?"

"I've heard that Grover Sparks had a sister. Do you know what happened to her?"

"Sure do. She got married, had a kid."

"Does she still live in town?"

"Sure does. Can't recall her name right now, but she lives up on Laurel. What'sis all about? You with the IRS or somethin'?"

"No, I'm a distant relative of Grover's. I'm looking up members of the family."

"Which Grover? My dad?"

"No, Sperks."

"I *am* Sperks."

"I mean, *Sparks*! I'm a cousin of the Sparks family."

"All mixed up, aint'cha?"

"Yes, but I'll straighten it out. Thanks a lot for your help. Goodbye."

"Don't mention it. Keep your nose clean. Hope, for your sake, the rumors ain't true."

"Thank you and goodbye. What rumors?"

"That Grover Sparks killed J. F. Dulls."

"What? I thought you said Grover Sparks killed himself."

"He did."

"So . . ."

"So what? You don't think the deceased can come back for revenge? You never met my Aunt Lucille. She's been haunting this house for twelve years jest 'cause I stole two quarters from her when I was six. And old Grover had plenty of reason to come back and take J. F. with'm. Ask his sister, you'll see what I mean."

61

"Lee Beagle?" you inquire.

"Sam?"

"No."

"Oh."

"Is this Lee Beagle?"

"Yes."

"Mrs. Beagle . . ."

"Ms."

"Yes, of course. Ms. Beagle . . ."

"Yes?"

"I'm calling from the president's Task Force on Business Integrity. As you may know, J. F. Dulls, one of the leading businessmen of Dullish County, recently died—"

"At 8:34 this morning."

"Precisely. In light of his sudden demise, we're conducting a survey to find out if certain allegations—"

"I don't know anything about it."

"Well, we've heard that—"

"About me? Did someone give you my name? In connection with J. F. Dulls? It's ridiculous, preposterous. I hardly knew him."

"We're not investigating you, Ms. Beagle—"

"Investigating? I thought you said this was a survey, not an investigation."

"It's an inquiry, Ms. Beagle, into J. F. Dulls's business practices and—"

"I had nothing to do with his businesses or his practices. He was my employer, that's all. I handled some of his accounting. I was paid by the hour."

"Yes, we know that, Ms. Beagle. That was at Dulls Gas & Electric Company?" you say, taking a wild stab.

"Who gave you my name?"

"State Employment. Standard procedure. Ms. Beagle, let's get right to the point. Was J. F. Dulls a crook or not?"

"He ... uh ... um ... he ... Do I have to answer these questions?"

"No. This is completely off the record, informal, and loose as a goose, Ms. Beagle. We're only trying to pull together a very broad picture for our report to the president and we're contacting anyone who had any kind of—"

"Did you talk to Sam Terene?"

"Who was that?"

"Never mind."

"Oh, yes, Sam Terene. He's on our list to call next. We figured he might know a thing or two."

"Then you haven't spoken to him yet?"

"No. But we will. Is he still—"

"No, we called it off. But we're still dating."

"I meant can he still be reached at ... at ..."

"Dulls Gas & Electric."

"Right!"

"Yes, he's still the manager. Maybe you'd better ask him your questions. Yes, that would be a good idea. I can't really help you. I'm very busy right now, and I don't know anything, and I'm not feeling very well, and I have to get off the phone and lie down. I'm sorry. Goodbye."

63

"You have reached the home of Edwina Gantry. Mrs. Gantry is not at home presently. If you would like to leave a message for her, please wait until the beeptone and do so. You will have thirty seconds for your message. Beep."

"Hi there," you say, trying to sound as friendly as possible on the tape, "I'm from the National Archives. Your name was given to us by J. F. Dulls—"

"Good lord!"

"Hello?"

"Why would J. F. Dulls want to give you my name, for heaven's sake?"

"He knew you, didn't he?"

"He knew everyone in Dullsville. And *everyone* knew him. Which is the reason for my little ruse."

"You mean screening phone calls with your answering machine?"

"I don't have an answering machine. I have been trying all morning to avoid this unnecessary prattle over the death of J. F. Dulls. I've gotten more than twenty calls in the last two hours regarding this episode. It's quite ridiculous."

"And why is everyone calling you, Mrs. Gantry?"

"Everyone is calling everyone. The phone lines are filled with rumor and gossip and idle defamation. The consensus from my little survey suggests that J. F. was murdered by one of his numerous enemies."

"Aha! Now we're getting somewhere. Did you ever work with J. F. Dulls?"

"God forbid! The man was a menace, a common crook. His poor brother Willard could tell you stories to make your hair part."

"You think Willard did the old man in?"

"Ha! Poopsy . . . that is, Willard . . . couldn't harm a flea. Even after all the years he suffered at the hands of that wretched man, he still was in tears over his death when I spoke to him today. Imagine, after stealing his wife and not giving him a single cent in all these years. And still Poopsy grieved for him."

"Then Poopsy won't be getting any bucks out of the estate."

"No. It will all go to that quack of a surgeon, Dr. Barton. There's justice for you. A drug pusher and drunk will inherit all of J. F.'s fortune while Poopsy, his own brother, who has worked and slaved all his life will get nothing. It's enough to make you resort to profanity."

"Are you sure Barton gets all the goods?"

"That's what Mr. Case told Willard. He said that Barton's taken care of if J. F. gets sicker. What else can that mean? And Mr. Case is J. F.'s lawyer, so he should know. Now, my dear young thing, if you will excuse me, I simply must get some rest. This frantic burst of telephone calls has left me quite out of sorts."

65

The busy signal is an annoying little invention, you decide. Like a brat having a tantrum, it wails relentlessly, never modulating, never missing a beat. You try the number three times, four times, and realize that some crucial conversation is in progress, full of key clues, but the irritating buzz in your ear convinces you that the call simply isn't worth the effort. And so, back to the Directory to follow a different lead.

68

"This is Marty Wince. I'm out of town until April third. If you'd like to leave a message, please wait until after the tone and speak clearly into the phone. You'll have about thirty seconds. If you're calling to leave an anecdote or joke about Dullsville in response to my advertisement, please call the library between the hours of 10 and 2 on Thursdays and leave it with them, along with your name. Thanks for your help."

71

Early telephones had hand cranks on the side, as seen in a dozen old movies. You recall reading that, contrary to popular thought, the crank didn't turn on the phone. It was simply a device that turned a generator inside the box, which, in turn, lit a lamp at the central operator's desk, signaling her that you wanted to place a call. That was in the days when people ran the phones.

These idle thoughts run through your mind as you sit, and sit and sit, listening to the endless sound of the ringing at the other end of the line. In the days of the crank, the operator would apologize for your delay, suggest calling later. She would commiserate, soften the rejection. But now that circuits, switches, and diodes are in control, there is no comfort. Just you and the pointless ringing in your ears and the cold fact that no one is going to pick up the phone and answer. Not now, not ever.

73

"Vic Bonsalvo speaking."

"Mr. Bonsalvo, this is Inspector Lestrade from—"

"Scotland Yard!"

"What?"

"You know . . . Lestrade. From the Sherlock Holmes stories."

You knew you had heard the name somewhere before.

"Not *Les*trade," you say, trying to cover up the oversight, "*Des*trade. From Cityville Homicide. We're looking into the death of J. F. Dulls."

"Think he was bumped off, huh?"

"We'd like to know what *you* think."

"Am I a suspect?"

"This is just an inquiry, not a formal investigation."

"Off the record?"

"All right."

"J. F. Dulls was one of the greatest men of the century in my book."

"Pretty small book, Bonsalvo."

"He made this town. He gave me my first job at DTS, then made me the head of the company. Sure, people think the trash business is just a lot of crap, but we've got plans for expansion and new ventures. DTS is going to be one of the major players in county trash in the next few years. Just wait and see."

"Some people think there was a little hanky-panky going on over at DTS."

"My wife tell you that? There's nothing between me and Lola. We're just a pair of friends."

"I'm talking about business practices, Bonsalvo. Come clean. Dulls ran DTS like his own private fiefdom."

"Who're you calling dumb? Look, pal, trash is a dirty business. Whatever Dulls did, he did for the good of the company and the good of the town. Did Ruby tell you all this? He's had it in for Dulls from the beginning. I told him to keep a lid on all his stories. Him and his secret notes."

"Secret notes?"

"Never mind. Let's just say that Ruby's got a good imagination. Dulls was good to me. Sure, he stepped on toes. But he took care of his own people. I'm not saying any more until I talk to a lawyer."

74

"Hello?"

"Hello, is this Willard Dulls?"

"Hello? Anyone there?"

"Hello! I'm calling from the—"

"Halloo!"

"Yes, hello to you, too. Mr. Dulls, I'm from the—"

"What the hell. Hello, hello?"

"Can you hear me?"

"Speak up, can't hear a thing."

"Hello!"

"Zat you Edwina?"

"No!"

"Can't find the battery for m'hearin' aid. Stone deaf. Damnedest thing."

"I'm not Edwina!"

"Have t'call you back, Poops. Sounds like a tunnel, can't hardly hear myself breathin'. It's gotta be here somewhere."

"Wait," you shout, but the sound of your voice seems to echo endlessly in a strange telephonic limbo.

76

"Is this Breede Case, the attorney?" you ask.

"Yes, it is."

"Are you the attorney for J. F. Dulls?"

"I am. What's the problem?"

"No problem at all, Mr. Case. The Cityville Center for Orphans and Widows is trying to find out if J. F. Dulls left us anything in his estate as he promised to do."

"Jumping the gun a bit, aren't you? He only died this morning."

"We know, but you see we have a terrible situation here at C.O.W. that has to be resolved today. We're reviewing a very sad case involving an entire family of orphans and widows. Sixteen people all together. A real tragedy. Frankly, we don't know if we can handle it on our limited budget. We were hoping to get some indication about the distribution of J. F.'s estate so that we could give these poor souls some hope."

"It's a private matter that will be handled in due course by the family's lawyer."

"Just a hint, sir? If you could only see those faces,

those pleading yet trusting little faces, looking to us for help and comfort in their most urgent hour . . ."

"Are you for real?"

"Mr. Case, you don't know what a frail thread life is to those without homes or families, without any means of support, a frail thread sewn into the fabric of circumstance."

"I thought you said this *was* a whole family."

"But destitute, Mr. Case, lost in the raging sea of indifference, cast aside by the great ship of society, and plunged into the topsy-turvy—"

"All right, enough! He didn't leave you any of his money. Okay? There's no mention of you anywhere in his will."

"He left it all to Barton, that fink!"

"Dulls left all his money to a foundation with strict provisions about taking care of the township of Dullsville for many years to come. He left nothing to any individual. He didn't leave any to you, or me, or to his doctor."

"But we've heard from Willard Dulls that Dr. Barton was to benefit."

"How the hell would Willard know a thing like that?"

"He said *you* told him. You said that 'Barton's taken care of if J. F. gets sicker.'"

"That old coot. Willard's deaf. What I said was that Barton was taking care of J. F.'s ticker. His heart! Is that all?"

"Alas, there are still the orphans to consider, sir."

"Great. Why don't *you* consider them. Do you mind if I get back to work? I've had enough of you and your sad cases for one day."

"Yea, though thou hast cast a cold eye to the plight of the wretched, yet will ye come to the mountain and say, Behold thy . . . Hello? . . . Hello? . . . Mr. Case?"

But the lawyer has hung up on you, leaving you to finish your biblical babble alone before your reflection in the computer screen, which seems somewhat perplexed by the harangue.

77

"Dulls Telephone. Mr. Hook speaking."

"Hello there, my name is Dusty Flores," you say, fumbling for a new identity. "I'm from the Union of Custodians. We're trying to—"

"What union of custodians?"

"The Cityville Union of Custodians, Chapter F-11. We're trying to—"

"Cityville? But you're calling from here in town."

"I am? I mean, yes, I am. But how did you know that?"

"This is the phone company, friend. Your call didn't go through the outside operator."

"Oh, well, as I was saying, I'm calling as the local Dullsville representative for the Union of Custodians. We're trying to locate one of your employees. Is there a man named Cleve working for the Dulls Telephone Company?"

"Why?"

"Because it seems he's overpaid his dues for the year and we owe him a refund."

"I see."

"I tried the number listed in the Directory, but there was no answer."

"Cleve's a little hard to reach, in more ways than one. He doesn't like people too much. He's a little shy, a little weird, too."

"Well, I'm sure he'll want to talk to me. We've a fat little check made out in his name. Is there any way for me to get in touch with him?"

"Well, if there's some money involved, I guess he would want to know. Can't you just mail the check? Send it to me at this office. I'll see that it gets to him."

"Sorry, I need to confirm some information with him first. Can't just be sending checks out like phone bills, now, can we?"

"I suppose you're right there. Hold on a moment, let me see what I can do." As you anxiously wait, you can hear the manager's muffled voice speaking to someone in the background. "Maggie, do you know if Cleveland's upstairs? I've got someone trying to reach him. Yes? Okay, I think I've got him for you," the manager says, returning to the phone. "He's not down in the custodian's room. He's up in his apartment. He's got a private number there that's not listed in the book."

"What's the number?"

"Now that you mention it, I haven't seen much of Cleve for the past few weeks. Seems like he's been working on something up there. He's kind of a tinkerer. When he's busy like that, he hardly takes care of his custodial duties. But J. F. never wanted to get rid of him. Don't know why."

"Can you connect me with him?"

"What do I sound like, a phone operator? This is a business office, friend. You'll just have to hang up and dial his number."

"Fine. What *is* the number?"

"But let me give you a word of warning. Cleve don't talk a hell of a lot. If you need information from him, you'd better have a bucketful of patience."

"Thanks. Thanks for your help and for the advice. Now, if you'll just tell me what the number is . . ."

"He's sure going to need some extra money. I doubt that the folks from Intercity will be keeping him around."

"How's that?"

"Intercity Phone. Now that J. F.'s gone, they'll be coming in to take over the phone system for sure."

"How do you know that?"

"Everyone knows that. We were talking about it for weeks here in the office. With J. F. gone, the deciding vote passes to Hillary Dill, the town controller. She's all for change, thank heavens."

"You're happy about the takeover?"

"You bet! I'll get a nice severance and I can go ice fishing all winter. Feel bad about Cleve, though. This phone system is sort of his whole life. Lives upstairs, never goes out. I'm sure the new managers won't want a sad old ghost like him lurking around."

"Don't hang up! Tell me the number first."

"I can't just tell it to you. Cleve'd be real pissed off about that. He can be pretty strange. I never give out his private number."

"Somebody must call him. How would he know *you* gave it to me?"

"Let's just say he has the capability up there to listen in on the phone lines."

"So how do you expect me to get in touch with him?"

"Let's just say his number is the one that takes the least effort to dial on a rotary phone, and leave it at that."

78

"Hello? This is Bonnie Tulle."

"Hi there, I'm a friend of Myna Rowell. She mentioned to me this morning that you had heard from—"

"Oh, you must be Edgar Poole's cousin, the one staying at his house for the season. How do you like the winter in Dullsville? Not quite what you expected, I'll bet. Edgar told us you were a mystery writer. Well, you're sure going to have plenty of time to write up here. You know, I've dabbled around with some writing myself, not the Great American Novel, but stories for magazines. I haven't had much luck with them, but I'm sure sooner or later—"

"Yes, I'm sure you will," you say, taking advantage of a short gasp for breath. "I wanted to ask you a question. Myna said you heard from a friend in the sheriff's office that—"

"Oh, about J. F. That was terrible news, wasn't it? Poor old J. F. But, of course, he did live to a ripe old age and, God knows, that's better than dropping dead at forty-five. Of course, I'd rather drop dead at forty-five with one hundred million dollars in the bank than live to ninety-six with nothing. But I guess I don't have that choice, so it doesn't matter very much, does it?"

"Right! Bonnie, did you hear anything else about J. F.'s death, any details about it or any—"

"Well, it's very strange because Millie—that's Millicent Storch, she sometimes works for the sheriff as a bookkeeper and happened to be in the office for a while this morning—she said that J. F. died while he was on the phone. Now that's pretty strange, don't you think, because why would a ninety-six-year-old man be on the phone at 8:34 in the morning? 8:34...that's the exact hour that he had his heart attack. And then Millie told me that the sheriff was very busy this morning checking into some crime that took place yesterday. Let me tell you that I put two and two together and I think—and this is just my own little theory, mind you—I think that J. F. was making some shady business deal, something he's no stranger to, and got some kind of bad news on the phone and that's what caused his heart attack."

"Shady business deal?"

"Oh, you're new here and not too familiar with our great founder John Foster; but let me tell you that he wasn't the paragon of virtue some people would like to think, and if you don't believe me you could just ask Billy Evans down at Dulls Propane, because he knows just what I'm talking about, or even Millie Storch— she'll probably be home by now—about some of the antics old J.F. was up to. You'd be surprised at how many people are completely ignorant of the—"

"That's very interesting, Bonnie, and thanks a lot for your help."

"Oh, I don't mind setting the record straight where J. F. Dulls is concerned. I know a lot of people are afraid of him and his money, but let me tell you—"

But she can tell you nothing because you have already hung up the phone and are deep into the Dullsville Directory again.

126   ALAN ROBBINS

80

The call to the custodian begins in the normal way, the number registering one by one in the earpiece; but it soon enters a strange limbo where it is met by total silence. No ring, no busy signal, no voice. You try the number twice more with the same result... an enticing stillness that suggests that you may very well be on the right track, temporarily blocked by a final effort at deception on the part of the murderer.

81

"Cleve, is that you?" the voice asks before you have a chance to say anything.

"Uh-huh?" you mutter, hoping to trick some answers from the responder.

"Listen," she continues in a whisper, "Clark has to go into Cityville this afternoon. He won't be back until next week because of the snow. This is our chance. I can't meet you here though; my mother's with us. Meet me at J. F.'s guest house after four o'clock. I have a key. I'll have to use the snowshoes, but it will be worth it. I can't believe we finally have this chance. Uh-oh, Clark's coming. See you later."

82

"Elihu Wharfe."

"Elihu Wharfe?" you echo.

"Speaking."

"Is this Elihu Wharfe?"

"This is Elihu Wharfe."

"Ah, Mr. Wharfe ..."

"Speaking."

"Mr. Wharfe ..."

"Who is this?"

"Mr. Wharfe ... this is Pease of the law firm Pease and Cannes. We're looking into certain allegations that ... Hello? Mr. Wharfe? Hello?"

But Wharfe has hung up on you, and repeated efforts to call the number again only result in an endless string of busy signals.

83

"Inez?" says the man who answers the phone, in a hush.

"Shhh!" you whisper, playing the game and hoping that it leads to some clues.

"You can't talk? Is Clark around?"

"Mnnn."

"Oh. Well, I'm glad you called. Listen, I've got to see you. Can you get away? Give Clark an excuse. Say you have to go up to the Wide House on council business. I know it's a long trek in the snow, but it'll be worth it, I promise. I'll meet you there later this afternoon, at the guest house. You still have the key, don't you?"

"Mmmm."

"Great. We'll finally be together. It's been driving me crazy. All these weeks without you. I can't stand it anymore. Do you feel the same way, my pumpkin?"

"Mmnn."

"God, I love it when you mumble. All right, my tomato, I'll see you later. And I'll be bringing Mr. Cucumber along, too. Kiss, kiss."

"Mnn-mnn."

86

Back in the good old days, the telephone was an amusing little thingamajig. Nothing but exposed wires and old magnets, held together by wax, gumption, and faith. Like any good clown, the magic was always one step away from disaster.

But now, a century later, it had grown up callous, tough, and unbreakable. It would, for example, ring for eons relentlessly and never give up. Nothing funny there. The real tragedy of the modern world, you decide, is that high-tech gizmos have absolutely no sense of humor.

Perhaps you have hit on something really significant while the phone continues to ring and ring. But probably not. In a moment you will come to your senses, forget these idle insights, and realize a more basic truth: No one is answering your call.

88

"Hello?"

"Is Dr. Barton there?"

"No, I'm sorry. This is his home number. You can call him at his office at number 21. Okay?"

"Is this his wife?"

"No, I'm his daughter."

"I see. I'm an old friend of his, from medical school. I was just calling to find out how this whole J. F. Dulls thing was going to affect his work. You know, we talked many years ago of opening a practice together. Do you know what his plans are, now that J. F. is gone?"

"He's probably going to retire. I hope—oh God, I hope—we'll finally move out of this dump and into the city. I mean this town really is dullsville. Okay?"

"Did your father have other patients besides J. F. Dulls?"

"No. Not in a long time. J. F. Dulls was enough for a whole hospital staff. Everything was going. It had to happen sooner or later. And sooner is better."

"Why is that? What difference would it make?"

"Oh, I'm sure Daddy was rewarded very nicely in J. F.'s will for all his years of devoted service. Daddy and Elihu were probably left all his money. He didn't trust his staff and he hated his family. I can't wait to get out of this dump. Listen, I've got to run... *The Young and the Restless* is on the tube. Call Daddy at the office if you want, okay?"

"Greta? Is that you?" says the person answering the phone.

"No. Is this Pinky Dulls?"

"Who are you? What do you want?"

"I'm calling from the Wide House. We're contacting all of the relatives of John Foster Dulls to inform them of the tragic passing, at 8:34 this morning, of Mr. Dulls."

"What?"

"The tragic passing?"

"What are you talking about? What are you saying? It's done already? But I didn't give the okay, I didn't give the go-ahead! My goddamn phone's been out of order until a few minutes ago. I never gave the code word. I never said 'Burnout'! What the hell is going on? Who gave the go-ahead?"

"Which go-ahead is that, Mr. Dulls?"

"Christ! Forget it, I'm just upset. I don't know what I'm talking about. You say my uncle died this morning? Did everyone else escape from the fire? Was anyone else hurt? Is Greta Wince all right?"

"Fire, Mr. Dulls? Who said anything about a fire? J. F. died of a heart attack."

"*What the hell is this, some kind of prank?* Are you working with Snitchit? What is this, some kind of extortion deal? Is that it? Where is he, where's Snitchit? Is he back at the office? I'll straighten this out. No one makes a fool of Pinky Dulls without his permission."

"Mel Snitchit?" you ask, finding the name in the Directory.

"Don't give me that crap. You're his little messenger, aren't you? If he's back at the Firewood office, maybe I'll pay him a little visit with my shotgun and we'll see about this extortion business. Heart attack, huh? We'll see who's going to have a heart attack!"

92

"Lang-a-lang-alang. Lang's TV."

"This is the Consumer Complaint Bureau calling."

"Look, haven't you guys bothered me enough?"

"We have?"

"Christ. Mulltown's nuts. I hike up there through the goddamn snow, fix the goddamn TV, adjust the antenna, hike all the way back and it's not enough that she calls me every day to tell me she's getting signals from Mars, but now she's got the FCC, the union, and . . . who did you say you were?"

"The CCB. Consumer Complaints. But—"

"Yeah, now you're gonna bust my hump. Look, the old broad's crazy, a nut case. She's got a little static because the wires in her house are as old as she is. Now, what the hell am I supposed to do about that? Give me a break! Signals from goddamn Mars?"

"We're not calling about signals from Mars."

"No? What's she got now? Lincoln's assassination on channel six?"

"We're not calling about any complaints about you.

We're trying to find someone who knows something about a Telepulse machine."

"Telepulse? You mean that pacemaker contraption up at J. F.'s house?"

"Exactly. We're looking into any role it might have played in J. F.'s death. We need an expert."

"His death, huh? You think the machine malfunctioned?"

"What do *you* think?"

"Couldn't say. Don't know a thing about it. TV's my game. You want to call an electronics man. Try AA. Or try Bolt. And if you get a call from a woman named Agnes Mulltown complaining about her TV repairman, tell her to go stuff it, okay?"

94

"Huh?" answers a groggy voice at the other end of the line.

"Hello?"

"What time is it?"

"Who is this?"

"Must have fallen asleep. Oh, God, my hair is going to look like hell!"

"Isn't this the garbage company?"

"Oh, sorry," she says, clearing her throat. "Dulls Trash and Scrap. Trash is our middle name. May I help you?"

"Are you sure?"

"We're kind of closed for the winter. Don't get too many calls after November. Look at this, it's all kinked up on the side."

"Kinked?"

"My hair. I slept funny."

"Look, I'm trying to get in touch with Victor."

"Who?"

"The guy who runs your company."

"Oh, Vic! Well, he wouldn't be here! Why would he be here? What makes you think he's here? Who are you, anyway? Do you work for his wife? Did she hire you?"

"Nobody hired me. This *is* his office, isn't it?"

"No, it's my home."

"But the number I called . . ."

"It's my home phone. We use it for the company during the winter. In case of emergencies."

"Do you get a lot of garbage emergencies?"

"No. You're not calling for his wife? That's a relief. Not that there's anything going on between Vic and me because there isn't. We're just a pair of friends. Listen, I've really got to go and shampoo my hair all over again. I look like I got a free haircut on Pluto."

"How can I get in touch with Vic?"

"Call him."

"Number?"

"It's in the book."

"Name?"

"The Dullsville Directory."

"Vic's name."

"Vickiebaby? Oh, you mean his last name so you can find it in the book, right?"

"Clever girl."

"Bonsalvo. Maybe I should just try to sleep on the other side so it looks balanced."

95

"Dr. Stone speaking."

"Hello, I'm calling from the county coroner's office. We're looking into the death this morning of John Foster Dulls," you say, trying to sound stuffy and professional. "You don't sound very shocked by that news."

"No, I heard about it from Stevie Weeks a few minutes ago. Stevie was also one of my patients."

"Aha! So J. F. Dulls was one of your patients."

"For many years. I'd say I've been up there treating him every Tuesday for almost a decade, I guess. Of course, less frequently in the winter."

"When were you last there?"

"Yesterday. It wasn't easy either. I had to get out my snowshoes and hike for two miles. But he had called to complain about some pain and I had to go."

"And do you think that this pain, or your treatment, in any way contributed to his death this morning?"

"I doubt it. I thought he died of a heart attack. I don't really see any way that acute molar odontaglia could contribute to a heart seizure. J. F. had a few worse problems than that."

"Such as?"

"Heart disease, weakening of the myocardia, periodic fibrillation. Plus the one thing that's sure to kill you off sooner or later."

"And what is that, Doctor?"

"Gerontitis."

"You seem to be quite the expert on the various ways J. F. Dulls might have died," you snort, thinking you have the cagey MD cornered. "And what is gerontitis exactly?"

"Old age."

"Oh. And this acute polar intaglio you've been treating him for every Tuesday? Fess up, Doctor, what is that exactly?"

"Toothache."

"Toothache?"

"Of course. That does seem to make the most sense, doesn't it?"

"Does it?"

"Well, I am a dentist, after all."

"You are? Then why don't you list DDS after your name in the phone book?"

"It makes my mother happy. She always wanted me to be a doctor. Besides, everyone in town knows who I am and I don't get many calls from other cities to trek over and fill a cavity. What's this all about, anyway?"

"I'll ask the questions, Doctor, if you don't mind. I don't suppose you know anything more specific about J. F.'s death," you probe, trying to salvage the phone call.

"Just what I heard from Stevie Weeks. What exactly do you want to know? Are you looking for medical information?"

"Exactly."

"Well, why don't you call Dr. Barton up at the Wide House? He's J. F.'s physician. I don't see what you expected to learn from his dentist."

"The coroner likes to be thorough, Dr. Stone. Dr. Barton is next on the list, and if I were you, I wouldn't leave town for the next few days. We may still have some questions to ask you!"

97

"Is Billy Evans back home yet?"

"No, he isn't. Are you one of his customers?"

"No, I'm not. I'm working with J. F. Dulls on a few business transactions and I have some questions for Billy. The name's Stock . . . man. Stockman."

"Billy's out on a call. I can have him call you back when he gets home—oh, wait a minute, I think that's him at the door. Billy? There's a call for you. Someone named Stockman, about J. F.," she says, and hands the phone over to her husband.

"Hi, what's the problem?"

"No problem, Mr. Evans. My firm—Stockman and Bond—is doing some business with J. F. Dulls and we're looking into certain—"

"Guess you didn't hear the news. I just heard it myself up at the Arlens'."

"What news is that?"

"J. F. died this morning. Hope that doesn't throw a wrench into the old works for you."

"My heavens, that's terrible news."

"Oh, yeah? You think so?"

"It puts an end to our negotiations. It's certainly bad news. But I take it that you don't agree."

"Look, it's none of my business, but if I were you I'd consider myself lucky that your deal has fallen through. Nobody knew the real J. F. unless they had a business deal with him. Believe me."

"You were his employee at Dulls Propane?"

"I was his boy, his lackey. He said jump and I jumped, that's all."

"Why?"

"He owned me, that's why. J. F. owned all the land in the area. Didn't you know that? And there was only one place you could get a mortgage to buy it from him: Dulls Equity and Loan. That's true for everyone in this town. If I didn't do exactly what he said, he could have us kicked out of our home, no questions asked. And he'd do it, too. You wouldn't believe some of the things he could do."

"For example?"

"For example, having old Mrs. Conkey thrown in jail for disturbing the peace because she wouldn't vote his way on the town council. Stayed in the jail for three weeks last winter, then went home and died, of shame probably. And who took her place on the council? One of Dulls's nephews."

"The sheriff went along with that?"

"That was Buster Croot, before Sheriff Shaffer. He was on J. F.'s payroll, like everyone."

"What did J. F. hope to gain by all this manipulation?"

"No comment. You want the lowdown on J. F.'s shady dealings, go call Stevie Weeks. He'll tell you. He's been trying to tell the state attorney for years. Unfortunately, the state attorney belongs to Dulls, too."

99

"Sheriff's office," announces the woman answering the phone at number 99.

"I'd like to speak to Sheriff Shaffer," you say, barely able to contain your glee at figuring out the puzzle.

"In connection with what?" she asks.

"The murder of John Foster Dulls."

"What was that?"

"That's right, I said the murder of John Foster Dulls. May I please speak to the sheriff? This is rather urgent."

"You *are* speaking to the sheriff."

"You're a woman?"

"If there's a murder in my jurisdiction, I'm a sheriff first and a woman second. Now, do you mind telling me exactly what you're talking about? You think J. F. was murdered, is that it?"

"I *know* he was. I mean, I'm not sure if I have proof exactly, but I think I do. I haven't had time to work out all the details, but I'm convinced that he was killed by a former associate of his, a man named Grover Cleveland Sparks."

There is a long silence at the other end of the line, like a jury taking their final secret ballot.

"Look, I don't know what you think you've come up with," she finally says, "or what kind of evidence you think you have, but my advice to you is to stop calling all around town and go back to your mystery writing."

"Hey, how did you know I was a mystery writer?"

"Word gets around. Now put down the phone and leave the nonfiction to professionals. Okay?"

"But I'm telling you, I've got information that proves it! First, Dulls ruined Sparks back in the thirties by stealing all his ideas. Second, Sparks is still alive and living above the phone company building in town. Third, Sparks knew that J. F. was going to vote down a proposition to bring in a new phone system. . . ."

"How would he know that?"

"Because he could tap into the phone lines any time he wanted. He listened in on the town; that's how he knew everything that was going on. Fourth, he built a device that interfered with Dulls's daily pacemaker test and killed him."

"Why would he do that?"

"I told you, so Dulls couldn't vote down the phone takeover. Sparks loved this town and wanted it to grow. He wanted everyone, himself included, to be free of J. F.'s iron grip."

"This is all crazy. You realize that, don't you? Murder by phone and all? Are you listening to yourself? If I were you, I'd hike down to the highway and hitch a ride to Cityville. I think you're getting cabin fever. It happens."

"Are you kidding? This murder has cured my cabin fever. Don't you think it's at least worth checking into?"

"First of all, Dulls's own doctor has already reported the death as a heart attack, natural causes."

"Reopen the case. He doesn't know what really happened. Sparks is an electronics genius. He killed Dulls without leaving a clue."

"Second, if Sparks is who you say he is, and if he did build such a device, then what makes you think it's still sitting on his desk tagged as Exhibit A?"

"All right, so maybe he dismantled it. But there's other evidence: receipts for the electronic parts, probable causes of death, motives..."

"You know what you sound like? A desperate writer searching for a plot. I don't know how this one will do in the bookstores, but it'll never make it in a court of law. There's no proof, no evidence, and it'll be April before anyone could conduct a normal investigation. So why not calm yourself down, make a nice hot pot of coffee, and go study the snow. I've got a real crime I have to deal with. Wen Gates threw his dog out of the house last night and it froze. So if you'll excuse me, thanks for the lead and don't call me again. Bye-bye."

The final click is more surprising than insulting, but you still find yourself cursing into the holes in the receiver. Without an outlet for your suspicions, you are forced to call Myna again to vent your excitement.

"Hello, Myna, it's me again. You're not going to believe this, but—"

"Oh, did you solve your murder mystery?"

"I certainly did. It's too long to go into now, but it involves a man named Grover Cleveland—"

"Sparks?"

"You know about him?"

"Everybody knows who he was. He and J. F. were business partners. He died back in the forties."

"No, he didn't. He's still alive. He's the custodian at Dulls Telephone Company."

"You mean old man Cleve? That's Grover Sparks? How'd you find that out?"

"Never mind that now. The point is, he killed J. F. Dulls!"

"No!"

"Yes. But when I told the sheriff the whole story, she wouldn't do anything about it, wouldn't even check into it!"

"That figures."

"Why? Isn't the sheriff supposed to be on the side of law and order?"

"Whatever Sheriff Shaffer is *supposed* to be, she is first of all Grover Sparks's niece. Her mother Lucy was Sparks's sister."

"*Is* his sister. No wonder the sheriff wasn't surprised when I told her Sparks was alive. She's obviously known all along."

"No kidding? Cleve is really Sparks? That's exciting. He's been quite a legend around here. Look, dear, the sheriff isn't going to do anything about your theory. J. F. is dead, he was ninety-six, things will go on. Frankly I think the new phone system is a good idea and so are all the other changes that are bound to happen. It's about time. Why don't you just drop the whole thing? It's all for the best."

"But we're talking about murder here."

"Justified . . . if what you say is true."

"I thought you liked J. F."

"I admired the man. I only liked his money. Besides, when a ninety-six-year-old man is murdered, it's more like a favor than a crime, don't you think?"

"I don't know; it doesn't seem right. On the other hand, J. F. made all his money at Sparks's expense; maybe he had it coming. There's only one thing I can't figure out. Dulls must have known who Cleve was. Why did he let him stay around?"

"To keep an eye on him? You said yourself he wanted to control everybody."

"But he had already ruined Sparks. The damage was all done. Why would he need to keep an eye on him? Unless there was something else, something he didn't want Sparks to find out. What do you know about the fire that killed Sparks's family?"

"I've never heard of that. If you need some history, why don't you call Marty Wince at the Historical Society?"

"But this must be something Dulls has kept secret all these years. The town historian probably wouldn't know."

"Wait a minute . . . I've got a better idea. If you think you know what it is, call Edwina Hobswerth. She was around in the beginning when Dulls and Sparks were first starting out. She might be able to confirm or deny your guess."

"Good idea."

"Tell me, what are you going to do about these—what do they call them on TV—allegations?"

"I don't know yet. What's Edwina Hobswerth's number?"

"It's in the book."

SOLUTION:
Solving the Mystery
In Only Ten Calls

1. DR. BARTON . . . #21

After hearing from Myna, and deciding that a murder has been committed, you naturally call J. F.'s physician to find out the details of his death. The logical place to find him, considering that his patient has just died, is at his office in the Wide House.

2. *THE TOWN CRIER* . . . #53

Following Barton's suggestion, you realize that some history of the town will help your investigation. Knowing that Marty Wince is out of town because Myna already told you so, you call the next logical place to get the information: the town newspaper.

3. LUCY SPARKS SHAFFER . . . #05

Looking through the Directory, you see that the only Sparks listed is this middle name and assume that this is Grover Sparks's sister, now married, who would certainly have some helpful information.

4. BENNY FIRESTEIN ... #33

There are two possible numbers, but a bit of luck here leads you to the correct party, suggested by Lucy Shaffer, who will give you some idea of how the murder may have been committed.

5. BOLT ELECTRONICS ... #29

Reasoning that you need an electronics expert, not a TV repairman or an electrician, you reach this number and get two important clues: a suspect and something that suspect would have to know to have committed the murder.

6. DULLS TELEPHONE COMPANY, CUSTODIAN ... #80

A false lead, but perhaps further proof that you are on the right path.

7. DULLS TELEPHONE COMPANY, MAIN OFFICE ... #77

This is the logical number to try in order to reach Cleve. Who else, after all, would know where he is since no one else seems to know *who* he is?

8. CLEVE ... #11

The answer to the riddle is number 11, which is available from no other source than the previous call. Cleve's knowledge of the frequency completes your conviction. You have solved the crime and therefore call the sheriff.

9. THE SHERIFF'S OFFICE ... #99

Perhaps putting together the two last names, and the family tie between the sheriff and Cleve, you are not surprised that the sheriff will not act on your theory. The only mystery remaining is why Dulls kept Sparks around, and what secret he may have trying to keep from him.

10. EDWINA HOBSWERTH ... #38

With the news that Dulls may have *caused* the death of Sparks's family, the final piece is in place and you can sit back and celebrate your resourcefulness.

About the Author

Alan Robbins is a writer and graphic artist living in New York City. His puzzle designs have appeared in *Games* magazine. He is the author of seven books, including two other interactive mysteries: THE SECRET OF THE GOLD JAGUAR and ON THE TRAIL OF BLOOD. His other books for Ballantine include PUZZICLES and CUT AND CONSTRUCT YOUR OWN BRONTOSAURUS.

Attention Mystery and Suspense Fans

Do you want to complete your collection of mystery and suspense stories by some of your favorite authors? John D. MacDonald, Helen MacInnes, Dick Francis, Amanda Cross, Ruth Rendell, Alistar MacLean, Erle Stanley Gardner, Cornell Woolrich, among many others, are included in Ballantine/ Fawcett's new Mystery Brochure.

For your FREE Mystery Brochure, fill in the coupon below and mail it to: